Finding Refuge

Dear Bob –
Please share your story with the world –
many thanks for your legacy.

Shim.
Timiro

Finding Refuge

✦

My Journey from the Middle East to Michigan

A Novel

Shirin Kambin Timms with Parviz Kambin

iUniverse, Inc.
New York Lincoln Shanghai

Finding Refuge
My Journey from the Middle East to Michigan

iUniverse books may be ordered through booksellers or by contacting:

iUniverse
2021 Pine Lake Road, Suite 100
Lincoln, NE 68512
www.iuniverse.com
1-800-Authors (1-800-288-4677)

Because of the dynamic nature of the Internet, any Web addresses or links contained in this book may have changed since publication and may no longer be valid.

Certain characters in this work are historical figures, and certain events portrayed did take place. However, this is a work of fiction. All of the other characters, names, and events as well as all places, incidents, organizations, and dialogue in this novel are either the products of the author's imagination or are used fictitiously.

ISBN: 978-0-595-43908-9 (pbk)
ISBN: 978-0-595-68873-9 (cloth)
ISBN: 978-0-595-88230-4 (ebk)

Printed in the United States of America

To my parents, who breathed wind into my sails,

To my husband and daughter who remind me to set anchor,

And to refugees all the world over who inspire me to look for the rising sun.

Acknowledgments

I would like to thank my family, who immigrated to the United States from Iran and served as the initial inspiration for this story. I would also like to acknowledge the refugees I have had the privilege of working with over the years. From them I have learned about the power of perseverance and compassion and what it means to "soldier" for your child.

Next, my colleagues and friends at Sewing Circle: Shana, Ikram, Gillian, and Dikki, I could not think of a better way to spend my Fridays than with you and the women we have come to know.

I also want to thank Carrie Allen, Brad Densmore, Deborah Davies, and Christine Gergo, who suffered through early drafts of this work and offered invaluable advice and support. Too, there is Vincent Delgado, who not only encouraged me to keep writing, but who also first introduced me to refugee service work years ago. Your creativity, compassion, and commitment continue to inspire me.

Of course, without my father, Parviz Kambin, this book would not exist. Dad, thank you for the opportunity to learn about your life and experiences. And Mom, thank you for your patience and for teaching me the value of tolerance, without which nothing of meaning in my life would be possible. Finally, thank you Daryl, my partner in all things great and small.

In closing, thank *you* for taking the time to explore a part of the world and a population so often misunderstood or simply forgotten. We will pass a portion of the proceeds from this book on to refugees in need.

Finally, should you consider reaching out to newcomers in your own local community, we leave you with these words by Margaret Mead: "Never doubt that a small group of thoughtful, committed citizens can change the world. Indeed, it is the only thing that ever has."

Shirin Kambin Timms
May 2007

Prologue

Greensburg, Michigan
The 1980s

We must be willing to let go of the life we have planned,
so as to have the life that is waiting for us.

E. M. Forster

Across the table, and slightly to the left, I saw a set of brown eyes, tiny little almond-shaped eyes. Up they came over the table top, and down they went, just below the table's edge.

Up, and over in my direction, and then down again. I can still see the child's chubby little fingers turn white as she clutched the edge and held on. Piled on top of her head was a band of ringlets. Her hair was dark, but twisted through were lighter highlights the summer's rays had painted in. As she slowly made her way back up over the edge, her eyes danced and her face compressed in smile.

Interesting how, across cultures, all the world's children love to play peek-a-boo. They so delight in discovering how someone can be present one moment and then turn hidden the next. Perhaps this is life's way of giving the little ones a hint? A hint about how life works, a hint about what is to come. Perhaps it is a way to whisper a clue, a message about how much can change in an instant.

◆   ◆   ◆

While this little girl played, I sat in the shape of something resembling a circle. Surrounding me were women I would never have met had my life tuned out the way I planned. As I looked around at the Russian, Cuban, Vietnamese, Hmong, and Afghan women around me, I felt that feeling again. It's the one you get when someone has died. The one where you can't even remember what day it is, and yet others seem to be happily buttering their toast or trying on clothes at the mall. It's the feeling that stops the hands on the clock.

I knew people were talking around me, but their words slid by. I watched their lips move, their hands gesture, and while I knew "we" were having a conversation, I was in a haze. I imagined I looked disinterested, and I tried to bring myself back, but I couldn't.

So, I focused forward, no target in sight. Even the little peek-a-boo girl had tired of trying to keep my attention and moved on to fingering through the children's book at the end of the table. It was a pop-up book, but someone had long ago pulled off all the standing characters. As the girl played in my periphery, I told myself I had to blink so that it looked like I was with the group. Still not able to break my trance, I heard a question and felt a pat on my arm. Someone was talking to me.

"What is your name, and where are you from?"

Every "talking session" started with this question, and so I promptly answered my interpreter. This temporarily pulled me back.

"My name is Meetra, and I am from Iran," I answered.

Then the conversation turned away from me. Conversation shifted quickly in this group, though few of the women shared a native language. Despite our different nationalities, we were all members of "the Sewing Circle." Twice a week we would file in and begin our work on our latest garment, curtain, or bedsheet. We would select from the fabric that happened to be on sale that month and start working on our machines. The machines were lined up along narrow tables, and for two hours at a time, all you could see were needles racing up and down, mowing the material beneath them. Over the murmuring, there was some conversation, but by the time Spanish, Russian, Vietnamese, and Farsi melted together, it all sounded like gibberish. I guess this is why we sat close to those with whom we shared a common tongue. It was softer on the ears.

Following our sewing, we packed up our machines and stowed away our latest creations. Each of us had a small shelf at the center, and when the clock struck eleven, we meandered over to the cabinet and stuffed our garments inside. An amalgamation of color filled the space, as some women gravitated towards brighter colors with big patterns and others searched out muted tones they could sew into conservative fashions. I used to wonder how much our styles of dress were a reflection of our cultures and how much were just about us. As I looked down at my dark skirt and even darker top, I thought about what the woman who was folding up her new yellow dress thought about me. I questioned what my clothes told me about myself.

After pushing in the last piece of cloth and shoving the door closed, we were asked to sit around the table once again. This time it was to talk and drink tea. I later learned the US was largely a coffee-drinking nation, but for many of us, tea was both our custom and our passion. Each of us believed we had the answer to the perfect cup, whether this had to do with the ways we prepared it, the tea leaves we chose, or what we elected to place in the tea. From my Afghan friends I discovered that cardamom was the spice of choice. The sewing circle specialized in "Lipton," however, and so we stopped talking about our delicious teas then and there.

I was never quite sure why we all got together to talk after our sewing class, but it was the practice, and so I obliged. Each language group was supposed to have an interpreter, and some interpreters were more reliable than others. Anyway, the idea was for all of us, we refugees, to come together and talk about our experiences. English was the core language, the language into which all other languages were translated back to. In theory, we were supposed to communicate with one another, despite our various mother tongues. We were supposed to share, despite all that seemingly separated us.

We talked about lots of topics in this group. Sometimes the subjects were serious, which made sense since we had all fled war and persecution. Sometimes, however, the subjects were light and just plain silly. I remember one day we talked about husbands and how they think that as soon as they do one chore in the house they are liberated men who now share their wives' workload fifty-fifty. We all laughed at that one.

On this particular day, the counselor started the conversation by asking a Cuban woman what had brought her to Greensburg, Michigan. The woman replied, "I don't know."

Suddenly, there was an outburst of laughter and the discussion completely stopped. As I looked around the circle, I watched several women lift their delicate fingers over their noses and cheeks so as to hide their wide-open, laughing mouths. In fact, I too was struck by her confusion. I should have known better though, as this particular woman was known to "walk sideways." Yes, there we would be, going along in rhythm, when Mercedes would say or do something that would have us all suddenly going sideways with her. She always brought attention to herself, and most of us were not sure if it was intentional or not. It didn't hurt that she was a striking woman whose long dark hair grew in volume and waviness on humid days. Her skin was lighter, but her eyes were dark enough to hide her black pupils. When it came to fashion, she was modern and progressive in her dress, liking all the latest styles at the time like leg warmers, headbands, and frilly blouses. On special days, she showed up in pretty lingerie tops that she loosely covered with lacey shirts. In fact, it was her yellow dress I watched get folded into the cabinet. It was her dress that made me notice my own. And so, against the backdrop of her vibrant presence and her loud and easy laugh, Mercedes had once again succeeded in jolting us into our own confused state.

Ironically, I think Mercedes had shocked herself by landing in a small Midwestern town after having been born and raised in Cuba. After all, one does not usually relocate so dramatically. And perhaps like the rest of us, Mercedes never thought she would wind up here.

As I let her comment settle in, I felt myself falling back into the haze. Then it occurred to me: "If you were to ask me what brought me to America—what had brought me to *Greensburg*—my answer could quite easily be, 'I don't know.'"

Iran
Early to Mid-Twentieth Century

The family endures because it offers the truth of mortality and immortality within the same group. The family endures because, better than the commune, kibbutz, or class-room, it seems to individualize and socialize its children, to make us feel at the same time unique and yet joined to all humanity, accepted as is and yet challenged to grow, loved unconditionally and yet propelled by greater expectations. Only in the family can so many extremes be reconciled and synthesized. Only in the family do we have a lifetime in which to do it.

Letty Cottin Pogrebin

Chapter 1

She climbed up the side of the building adjacent to where he worked and slowly moved toward the edge of the flat roof. She was two floors from the ground. As she peered down, scanning the ground below, she searched for the right man. She had been told what he looked like, and she even stayed on the rooftop a few extra minutes hoping he was *not* the person she was spying on.

After about a quarter of an hour her stomach settled. She realized, without a doubt, she was eying the man she would spend the rest of her days with. Yes, *this* was the man she would have children with, and the man she would be hinged to for the rest of her life. This short, acne-scarred, balding man—seventeen years her senior—was going to be family tomorrow. He was going to trump all other family members, even the cherished mother and father she had known and loved since birth. Legally and emotionally, she would belong to him, the man she had only ever seen from a neighboring rooftop.

◆   ◆   ◆

This is how Maman always started her love story. As we would kneel around the coffee table dipping fresh bread into our hot glasses of tea, she would tell us about the day she stood on that rooftop on a stakeout in search of our baba, our father, whom she would marry the next day and later have five children with. We would always laugh as we pictured my five-foot-tall mother hoisting her dress and short legs onto the rooftop. To create a sense of suspense as she told the story, Maman would pause at just the right moments and pop a sugar cube into her mouth. She would then take a sip of tea from her glass, gripping the top edge ever so carefully so as not to burn her fingers. There she would be, sucking on the cube, as we waited for the rest of the story.

The truth of the matter is that the rest of the story is the story of our life. Of course, Maman's part started with her engagement to Baba and her journey to Tehran, where, years later, she would greet each one of us into the world, one wet, grinning face to another.

My mother was born and raised in Kashan, which meant she had to be transported north to Tehran in order to marry my father. With that, at the age of sixteen she was plunked into a horse and carriage with her one suitcase and driven to the city by my father's uncle. Tehran was more than a day away, and the route out of Kashan was windy, dusty, and at times desolate. Some patches, however, were peppered with low-lying, flat-roofed houses, overstretched clotheslines, and people just sitting around waiting for something to happen. Wherever the road cut through these small villages, the entire town came out to see who was rolling by. The onlookers, desperate for some new sight, sound, or smell, would literally come to the edge of the carriage, eyes squinting, and stare into the coach as mother wheeled along. One village woman even clasped Maman's bicep and then lifted her one eyebrow in approval. Maman told us the woman then turned to her husband to say something about how Maman was strong for her size and would be a good addition to the farm.

Later in the day, as the afternoon sun was fading, Maman pushed her veil back past her temples, turned toward the front of the vehicle, and yanked on the sleeve of Hassan, her chaperone. She sank her green eyes into his black pupils, knowing all the while she shouldn't be making such direct eye contact.

"*Bebakhsheed*, excuse me, would you mind if I came up and sat with you for a little while?" she asked.

"*Ah dokhtar*, young lady, *mardoom chee meegan?* What will people say?"

Maman lowered her head and felt her veil slide back down over her face, shielding the setting sun. As she rubbed her palm with her fidgety fingers, she knew what people would say. They would say that she was wild, that she was not from a good family, because she, a single woman, had been seen fluttering around town with an unmarried man.

Neither said another word until they stopped at a *Karvan-Sara* in a small village that night. The place was swarming with travelers, all of whom knew this was a good place to pause and get some rest. Everyone staying for the night was piled into a large, common room covered by a delicate, shaky roof.

Maman looked around. People were lying on the small Persian rugs they had brought for mats. Travel bags, also made of carpet, doubled as pillows and backrests. One strange face after another crowded her space. People were coughing, grumbling, smoking water pipes, and staring at one another past the point where anyone could say it was polite. The place smelled like a mix of mildew, body odor, and spoiled vegetables. As if that were not enough, Maman was so close to the person next to her that when he looked her way she could smell his garlicky breath. Maman knew she was among some who were en route for legitimate business and some who were not. Trembling and wide-eyed, she turned to her chaperone and whispered.

"I can't sleep here. Who are these people? What if they steal from us or hurt us while we are asleep?"

"It will be okay. Really. Just try and relax. Get some rest."

"I can't. I know I won't be able to sleep. Would you please hold my hand? *Please?*"

"*Ghorban*, take the end of my cane. I'll hold the other end. That's how you will know I am here." Hassan was sympathetic. Maman knew that there was not much more he could offer her.

Maman clutched the end of the cane and held its point close to her chest. For the rest of the night she stayed awake, making sure her chaperone never let go of the rounded edge of that lifeline.

With the light of dawn, Maman unshackled the cane from her clutching fingers, clambered into the back of the carriage, and continued her journey to Tehran. Once there, despite custom, and despite regard for what people might say, my sixteen-year-old mother decided once and for all she was going to get a glimpse of my father before she said, "I do." From there, she headed to the rooftop.

Years before Maman ever found her way to that rooftop, Baba had come to Tehran in search of work. That had been 1913. To the chant of *Allah-Akhbar*, he had watched his carriage pull out of Kashan, the same city his future wife would be from too. He remembered hearing the women yell out "God is Great" as they waved good-bye and wiped their teary faces with the ends of their headscarves. Baba would always remember that carriage, which was really only a horse-drawn platform lined with wooden rails. As he watched the passengers snake their skinny arms around the bars, and as the cart bump along the sandy, stony road, the pots and pans tied onto the rails for safekeeping clanged and clattered.

During the early part of the twentieth century, many Iranians, my father included, believed they were witnessing the emergence of a modern, even westernized, Iran. Under the reign of Reza Shah, my father took in the smell of fresh sawdust each day as he headed to work. Making a living buying and selling all the latest textiles, Baba would often catch his co-workers peeking around the bright rolls of fabric so as to get a glimpse of the women walking by. After all, by law, their faces could now surface from behind the veil. This was a time of transformation, both for my country and for my family.

◆   ◆   ◆

Soon after marrying, my mother began having children. I am the youngest of five and—if I have to be honest—I would have to say that most of my memories include only those shared by the bottom three of us. In other words, my two oldest sisters were grown and contemplating marriage when we bottom three were still spitting pistachio shells at one another.

My brother's name is Khosro. When we were not fighting, Khosro and I were good companions for one another. In fact, we were partners when it came to milky stove tops. You see, each week my mother set out to make yogurt, which involves heating a large pot of milk until it almost boils. Once sufficiently warmed, you add a few spoonfuls of already made yogurt, stir, cover the pot, and rest it in a warm place overnight. By morning, the mixture should be thick and ready to place into a porous cloth so that the excess water can drain. Easy.

The problem, however, came when Maman was waiting for the milk to simmer. You see, my mother was not a woman who liked doing one thing at a time. She would be working the stove, soaking clothes in the tub, rocking her baby niece's bassinet with her foot, and scolding Khosro and me with her wooden spoon.

This was all fine when she first lit the burner and started to warm the milk. Once the pot started to heat, however, it was a different story. Within literally a second, the milk would rise up suddenly and—as any distracted yogurt maker knows—boil, *bang*, over the top before Maman could catch it. Honestly, you have never seen a mixture change from one state to another so fast.

And so, Maman's multitasking always caught up with her no matter how hard she tried. As if that were not enough, Khosro and I would intentionally try to preoccupy Maman when we knew the milk had been on the stove for some time. The result? Sour-smelling, milky stove-tops were a standard feature of our household.

◆   ◆   ◆

When I think about Khosro, other stories come to mind as well. One day I came into the house and tripped over pieces of plywood. Just as I was about to plant down my foot anyway, I saw a small replica of the Eiffel Tower. It sat atop a miniature table that Khosro was getting ready to sell to the local toy shop. I decided to step carefully, even though we had fought the night before.

With a zigzag across the floor, I smelled sautéing onions and spotted my mother cooking in the kitchen that sat detached from the main house. As soon as I reached her and started to talk, she handed me a fistful of green beans to chop for the stew we were having that night.

As I started to cut off the dry, brown ends I said, "Maman, Khosro and Aram were playing *Zeshteh-ya-Mahe* again." I loved tattling on him.

As a semi-mature boy—"semi-" being the operative part of the term—Khosro and our cousin Aram would play a game in which they would scout out a veiled woman on the streets of Tehran and then place bets on whether she was pretty or ugly. Because the women had most of their bodies shrouded behind a chador, Khosro and Aram decided to look to the women's ankles for hints about their beauty. Their astute and scientific minds hypothesized that thin and pretty ankles meant she was pretty, and thick, "fat" ankles, translated to ugly. From there, they placed their bets accordingly.

Once they had ferreted out their chosen woman, they approached her and asked her a question. For instance, "Where is the local shoe store?" or "Where is such and such a street?" and so on. The boys hoped that the woman, provoked into responding, would shift her veil ever so slightly so as to reveal her face. The exchange between prey and predator was short, but once the innocent woman was on her way, Khosro and Aram would exclaim *"zesht!"*—ugly!—or *"mahe!"*—beautiful! News of this game always got my mother's cooking spoon shaking at the two of them.

"What? Where were they?" Maman barked back, as an onion crackled against a chunk of meat in the hot oil. I watched steam escape out of the pot and swirl around Maman's head, making the tiny strands of hair around the edge of her face fuzz up and curl.

"Down by the grocer. They got one of the Polish ladies today."

"Ugh, that child. Wait till I tell Baba." Maman then took a handful of the beans I had cut and dumped them into the pot with some tomatoes. "Hurry up, we have a lot to do today."

"Maman, why do the Polish ladies look so different?" I asked, pushing my knife faster.

"Because they are not from Iran. They are from Poland." At this point, the rice had boiled. Maman was draining it for its second bake. I watched her oil the bottom of the pot, line it with some sliced potatoes, add a few spoonfuls of water, and dump the rice back in. She was making our national favorite—*tahdig* and rice.

"Why did they come to Iran?" I asked, now with only a small pile of beans left to chop.

"They're refugees. During the war they were prisoners under Stalin. Then, when Hitler invaded the Soviet Union, Stalin released them so they could work with the British and form an army against the Germans. They came to Iran to get organized." She looked over at me. "Are you finished with the green beans?"

"Yes. I put them in the pot."

Maman added tomatoes, sprinkled the stew with some turmeric and cinnamon, and continued. "You should be careful of the refugees. They were so sick when they came here. The government quarantined them for a while because they had lice, typhus, and other problems. An epidemic still broke out though. That's why I am always telling you kids to keep clean."

"Did they fight in an army? Even the women?" I asked.

"I don't know. A lot of them died on the way to Iran or after they got here. Those who survived, most of them at least, moved on and settled in other countries."

"Why don't they wear a chador?"

"I don't think they are Moslem. They don't have to, anyway. It's not the law. Be careful—some of them play bad games."

At the time I didn't understand what Maman was talking about. As I grew older, I came to realize that while some of the Polish refugees worked in hospitals and served as secretaries and domestics, others worked the brothels. I am sure this was in part the result of the abuse they suffered in Stalin's camps, and in part the desperation and hopelessness they must have felt once in our country.

As for Khosro and Aram, the unveiled Polish women were a shoo-in for the game of *"Zeshteh-ya-Mahe."* With their faces open to the hot Persian sun, it was easy to tell if they were pretty or ugly.

◆   ◆   ◆

While my brother Khosro was happy to walk right on the line of life, my sister Irandokht always stayed between the lines. Irandokht was quiet and reflective, and she always looked neat. She regularly ironed her clothes and stayed out of the trees and mud. She loved to read, listen to music, and help my mother. I remember watching her sweep the floor and wash the dishes, and all the while I knew she was doing chores she hadn't even been asked to do. She was also the most soft-spoken in the family. From my mother on down, we were a pretty spirited bunch. I can't even remember Irandokht showing an unpleasant emotion. I am sure she must have had them, but I honestly can't recall her ever lashing out against anyone or anything. Usually, when she felt a strong emotion come on she got quieter instead of louder. The rest of us? We got louder. That's why she stood apart. She was the most religious of all of us too, so perhaps her passion for God influenced her temperament.

My earliest recollections of Irandokht are of how well she watched the pot while making yogurt. There she would stand, forgetting about the clothes in the tub, her crying cousin in the bassinet, and the circle Khosro and I were running around her. Hawk-eyed, she waited for the first frothy bubble to surface, and when it did she gently moved the pot from the flame. The "rise" subsided. No sour milk. No milky stove-tops. As for how Irandokht treated Khosro and me, it's fair to say that the answer is "just about as good as Maman." One day, during the *Nowruz* season, Maman had sent Khosro and me to the baker for some fresh pastries for the upcoming New Year's celebration. Our home was located on a long and narrow street that was only about eight feet wide. Twenty-five-foot walls lining the street concealed the brick and clay homes our neighbors lived in. During this particular New Year's season, the Tehran skies had been pouring out rain for days. In fact, by the time Khosro and I had started back to the house, our narrow street, once a dirt path, had nearly turned into a river.

For Nowruz, Khosro had gotten a new, freshly polished pair of brown shoes as a gift from Baba. Each morning as he knotted bows onto the shoes, he asked Maman what errands he could run for her. Although he thought we were all fooled by his generosity, the fact of the matter is that we knew Khosro just wanted to gallivant around town, showing off his new footwear. Against Maman's advice, Khosro had worn these very same shoes on the day we headed out for our baklava and sugar-coated, rose-flavored almonds. As he wound through the streets, jumping over one puddle only to land smack dab into another one, his luck soon turned, and he wound up ankle deep in mud.

Turning around, I watched him grip his thigh and yank his leg from the heavy earth. A naked foot emerged. Just as I was about to yell, "Hurry up! Maman is waiting for us!" I started to laugh. There Khosro was: all dressed up in his fancy, pin-striped pants and tailored navy shirt, shoeless and sockless. His bony, bare foot dangled above the mud, and his shoe was nowhere in sight.

When he looked up at me, his jaw dropped open. His face went pale. The rain kept pouring down on us, and the sugar on the almonds started to dampen and get sticky. Even though we were soaked through with water, I watched Khosro's face crease in distress and his chest heave in breath.

Not knowing what to do, he then lifted his other foot out of the mud. Immediately, this foot met the same fate as the first.

The more Khosro panicked, the harder it was for me to contain my laughter. By the time his second foot came out, toes fully extended in shock, I let the almonds fall to the ground and proceeded to wrap my arms around my waist and laugh out loud. With my head up and face to the sky, I witnessed Khosro go from pure distress into absolute rage.

Not knowing who darted first, we chased each other down the street. When we arrived at home, I was still laughing, and Khosro was still barefoot. Irandokht's response was typical of her: she wiped Khosro's tearful face, offered him a dry pair of socks, and went looking for the new shoes buried in the mud outside. Within minutes she returned, a clay-packed bundle with strings dripping from her wet hands. By that evening, Khosro's new shoes, sitting beside the rest of our family's footwear, were glossy enough to reflect the flame of the lamp Maman had lit in our living room. These are the kinds of memories that come to me when I think of my sister.

Chapter 2

During my childhood, few houses in Iran had any kind of centralized heat. Instead, houses had *kourseys*, which were coal-filled brass containers encased in wood. They sort of looked like short tables. Anyway, our koursey was covered over with a red and gold handmade quilt. Atop it sat a brass tray holding bowls filled with dates, raisins, and nuts for snacking. Around the koursey, Maman had placed large cushions that were covered in maroon, rug-like cases. We each had our favorite spot around the heater, and as we filed into the room like a line of matchsticks, we tucked our little legs under the blanket. Of course, for circulation purposes, Maman was always fanatic about making sure the window on the back wall was slightly cracked.

One day in early spring, Khorso, Irandokht, and I were under the koursey blanket, cackling about the day's events, eating pistachios, and supposedly doing our homework. Just when I would start to concentrate on adding up the long columns of numbers lining my sheet of paper, down came a pistachio shell, right into my notebook. One even wedged itself into the curly spiral. I remember hearing Khosro snicker and watching Irandokht smirk while she tried to keep her eyes on her work. To raise the ante, I decided to dig into the glass serving dish for an already plump raisin, dunk it into my hot tea to make it all the more sticky, and smash it into Khosro's writing assignment. I saw arcs, dots, and squiggles on his page and tried to aim the gooey raisin right into one of the bigger swishes he had copied from his grammar book. Maybe I hit an "n," or maybe it was a "j," letters which, when concluding a word in Farsi leave just enough room in their round bellies for something the size of a small raisin. Before my pressed finger left his page, I could see his forehead crinkle with worriment. Now, there was no way around having to rewrite his assignment. As I listened to him grumble and watched his pencil speed along, I could swear his *n*'s and *j*'s had shrunk.

Anyway, there we were, the koursey blanket over our little legs, working on the homework that was due the next morning. The sun was starting to go down, and the shadows in the room were growing taller. Every now and again, a ray would catch a shiny thread on the blanket and steal my attention away from the list of numbers in front of me. At the time, I didn't know where Maman was, although I suspected she was steaming the rice and beans we would be eating for dinner that night. I almost swore I smelled fresh dill as I added six plus four.

Ten minutes later, Maman came into the room and sat down beside Irandokht and me. As she made her way onto the floor, she looked at our notebooks as though she were checking up on our progress. Her eyes never made their way from right to left and back again, however, and this was my first hint something was wrong. Her hair had come loose from its braid and was all fuzzed up around her ears and temples. She looked like she had been outside scrubbing our grass-stained clothes in the hot Tehran sun. The strange part was, this early in the season the Tehran sun had not heated to its boiling point.

She had her knees close to her chest and her hands clasped around her shins. As she started to speak, I watched her relax her legs into an Indian style position, and slide the blanket over her lap.

As she played with some invisible lint on the blanket, she began to speak in a slow and steady voice.

"Children, I have something to tell you."

"Maman!" Irandokht gasped.

"It's okay, sweetheart, *azeezam.*"

Khosro and I looked to one another for clues. What scared me most was watching Khosro's dancing, playful eyebrows lower in fear. His lips then narrowed, and I could tell he was biting the inside of his cheek. I could not see Maman's face, but when I turned towards Irandokht I saw her staring forward, eyes filled. It was clear they both understood something I did not.

Soon, tears poured down Khosro's face too. My eyes shifted back and forth between all three of them, and then I felt my mother's hand on the base of my neck. My hair spilled over her wrist and forearm as she leaned in and kissed me on my cheek. I remember smelling the rose-scented cream she rubbed into her face each morning.

As she moved away, I watched a tear flow out of her eye and around the faint lines on her face. She had a dark mole on her chin, and when the tear reached its edge, the droplet disappeared.

I don't remember any of us talking, and I certainly don't remember eating the dilled rice and beans Maman had prepared for us that night. What I do remember, though, is that it was on that day I learned about the power of a single moment. I learned that while some changes occur over time, others work their way into our lives in only an instant. One minute the world is one way, and—literally—one minute later it is forever changed.

Yes, there are times in life when a day makes a difference, and with my father now having passed, this was one of those very days.

Greensburg, Michigan
The 1980s

Ideologies separate us. Dreams and anguish bring us together.

Eugene Ionesco

Chapter 3

It was Sewing Circle Friday, the day I regularly visited Second Chances, the Refugee Resettlement Office on the other side of town. Fall had left, and winter, an early visitor to the state of Michigan, had already lowered itself from the sky. As I opened my bedroom window to check the temperature, I could hear the whistle of tree branches slicing the thick wind. Yesterday's snow was still on the ground, but now parts of the driveway were edged by small mounds the plow-trucks had created following the storm. As I pulled the window back down and locked it, I couldn't help but think that I really just wanted to stay in my apartment and crawl back under the blankets.

I was now in Greensburg—certainly a safer place than others where I had lived, but it still felt foreign. I often felt as though I stood out. Despite having studied English in high school, I rarely understood what people were saying. The written word was easier for me to make out, but as soon as someone began to talk, it was as though all the spaces between their words and sentences disappeared. People's voices sounded like one long line of English sounds. Then, when their speech paused, it usually meant I was expected to offer an answer in return. I typically left most conversations feeling more isolated than I had felt when alone.

Life was physically hard as well. Living in the Midwest without a vehicle meant I had to walk most places that could not be reached by bus. I also happened to live in a section of town with few sidewalks and other pedestrian amenities. I could get to a supermarket in about eight minutes, though, and because my neighbors regularly left abandoned shopping carts outside our apartment building, I would always grab one on my way to the store. I only filled the cart half full with groceries, however; since I was still learning about American currency, I was perpetually afraid of running out of money.

Because my street was one of the last to be plowed in the area, snowy days, common in Michigan, were especially difficult to navigate with the shopping cart. Something that rolled along so readily on asphalt was most unresponsive in the snow. In fact, as I moved along, staking my feet into the ground so I could push harder, I found that more often than not I just had to stop so I could get the snow out of the clogged wheels.

One day, after cleaning out the wheels four times on the way back from the grocery store, I cried. I didn't think I was going to, but as I leaned down to push an icy mound out of the rubber circle, tears streaked my face. Like water on the loose, I felt anger seep all through my body, starting in my chest and then radiating out through my neck, arms, and legs. I felt my heart pound, my face heat, and my cheeks melt the falling snowflakes. As though they were no longer a part of me, I watched my gloves slide away and my red, raw hands bang against the wheel. When that didn't work, I stood and saw my foot kick the bottom of the cart, angled in such a way so as to access the crevices. As I watched my appendages work to release the snow, my mind numbed and then retreated. It went someplace else, and all I knew was that I was banging at something I feared I would never get ahead of.

My rage was interrupted by one of my neighbors flying out of the apartment complex with his child in tow. I heard the screen door on the front of the building blast against the wall, and as I looked up, one more hinge on the door pulled loose from the frame. As the screen ricocheted back, it no longer fit in the groove.

I didn't know this man, but I had seen—and certainly heard—him before. He had an explosive temper. Night after night, I heard him fighting with his girlfriend in the unit next door. Periodically, the police would come, but nothing was ever resolved. The next night they were at it all over again.

That day, as he blasted out of the door, he had his young son under his arm and was carrying the child to the car. The child kicked his feet and pounded his fists against his father's thigh. The father then opened the door to his rusty, dark blue automobile and literally threw the child into the back seat. As he slammed the door shut, he yelled out something I didn't understand. In response, the child bundled his arms and knees close to his chest, turned away from his father, and began to cry.

I looked down at my snowy cart, afraid my stare would catch the man's attention. I didn't want to be asked why I was interfering in his "family" business. As the rust-speckled car drove past me, I heard the windshield wipers screech across the glass, making the loud sound they always do when you first turn them on and the glass isn't wet enough to allow them to glide smoothly. I also heard a clanking sound coming from the engine. Just when I thought I could lift my head safely, I looked up, and—without intending to—looked right into the big, black eyes of the child. He saw my tears, and I saw his. We both started to cry harder.

◆   ◆   ◆

The Sewing Circle was in the basement of Second Chances. That day, the core group was there working on children's clothes, pillowcases, and new dresses. When the clock struck eleven, we all packed up our machines and moved to another table where we could sit in a circle. There were a few newcomers, so we all introduced ourselves, telling those who didn't know us what country we had immigrated from. From there, Melissa, one of the counselors, asked us how we were doing. Other than the little bit of information she shared with us, I never came to know a lot about Melissa. Apparently, she had been born in Michigan and was as "American as apple pie," she used to say. With her freckled cheeks and a button mouth, she grew up in a small, homogeneous town and then decided one day it would be exciting to move to Africa. With her parents pressing their befuddled faces against the airport windowpane, she waved good-bye and set out to make a difference. Once back in the United States, she studied social work and became the counselor in charge of our sessions. Each week she would greet us with a wide smile and a roll of fabric. She had learned our color and texture preferences and made a special effort to shop with each one of us in mind. Because of the language barrier between us, I didn't know much more than this. Oh yes, there was the coffee. A shiny paper cup with a red emblem on it was never far from her lips. The emblem matched the one on a card she showed one of the other women who regularly stopped at the corner café. "Make sure you get it punched each time," she would instruct.

In response to her inquiry as to how we were doing, Miriam, a Jewish refugee from Russia, started to speak.

"Ya, not feeling so good today."

"What's wrong?" Melissa asked.

"High blood pressure. It go up and down, but these days, it up more than down."

"Do you take any medication?" Mercedes, asked.

"I do it "Russia way." I take hawthorn berries for blood pressure and valerian root when I nervous or can not sleep. Helps with headaches too. No prescription medicine because it won't work when I really *need* it."

Melissa started to speak. "I'm not sure prescription medicine works like that, Miriam. I think doctors recommend you take it every day so it can work over time and gradually reduce your blood pressure. Taking medication inconsistently could cause you more problems."

"No, no. You are wrong! I should not take it too much. If I take it too much, how is the doctor going to know what my *real* blood pressure is?" The word "real" was punctuated by a loud sound. In a sort of inside-out clap, Miriam had slammed the back of her right hand against the palm of her left.

"What do you mean?"

"If medicine changes pressure's reading, then the doctor will only have a fake result. The medicine's number. Artificial number!" Miriam raised both eyebrows and looked at Melissa like she was an idiot.

Melissa's lips gently puckered as she listened to Miriam's explanation. You could tell she was trying to figure out how to counter Miriam's medical logic without being disrespectful or comic. As I looked around at the circle of women, many of whom were listening through their interpreters, I could see a break right down the middle. Some could plainly see Miriam's logic and nodded their heads in agreement. Others laughed outright at her rationale, and—more importantly—at the force of conviction Miriam exhibited.

Me? I could care less. I didn't like Miriam, which made it hard to think she could ever be funny. Of course, I didn't follow her logic much either. I remember thinking that I just wanted to go home, even if "home" these days was a place where raging neighbors took out their anger at the world on their little children.

"What about diet? You can sometimes impact your health by making the right dietary choices." Melissa was obviously trying to "make a difference" this week.

"Ah, ya! They want me to eat fruit and vegetables. *Five* a day! What am I? A monkey? That will make me sick. Sixty years I eat potatoes, sausages, and bread. This is good food. How are a handful of grapes going to fill me up? It's crazy. I no chimpanzee who is going to run around with a banana in my hand everyday!"

Once the interpreters had finished their translating, Miriam started up again. "You know, I don't understand why doctors don't visit sick people in their houses? In winter it bad to ask sick people to go to doctor's office! In Russia, doctors came to us. *This* is America?"

"Well, I can see where you are coming from, Miriam," Melissa started again. "But in this country it is customary for patients to visit the doctor's office. I can see where it can be hard though."

"Ugh. It is wrong!" Miriam pulled her styrofoam cup to her lips and drank. As she sipped, I hoped her tea would shut her up. I was growing tired of her medical narrations and her excessive demands. Perhaps, had she a softer side, a more diplomatic way of asking for help, she would have been a more sympathetic figure. Instead, she seemed to bark out criticisms, and when she needed something she would come right up in your face and essentially manipulate you into giving it to her by telling you that *you* didn't need it. For example, if she wanted a particular piece of fabric, she would come over, rub her chubby fingers across it, and tell you you had no use for it. She wouldn't even give you a chance to answer her before you would literally see the back of her flat head, bobbing away, cloth in hand. She also played favorites, and you quickly knew if you were one of them or not by the way she greeted you. If she pulled you into her fat bosom for a hug, you were in. If you got a grunt or were totally ignored while she pulled the person next to you into her oversized bust, you were out. I was out.

Miriam had an interesting story. It was just a shame she was the one who had to tell you about it. Miriam had come to Greensburg with her husband a year before. She could talk at length about the Jewish experience under Soviet rule. Not surprisingly, she had nothing positive to share. She blamed much of the loss of Russian Jewish identity on communism. Miriam never really talked about any persecution she directly endured, but it was clear she was depressed. However, when Melissa suggested that maybe she talk one-on-one with someone, Miriam realized Melissa was talking about counseling. We had to push down the hair standing straight up off her head.

"Counseling! You crazier than me? I know *all about* counseling, for sure. Yeah, the Soviets were famous counselors. They counsel the spirit right out of you. Make you into a good little communist. Ha, if *you* think...."

Soon, she was saying the same thing over and over, just louder and louder. In what seemed like a simultaneous outburst, both Melissa and the Russian interpreter, known for her calmness and objectivity, shouted, "Okay, okay. Forget it! No counseling!"

In fact, this was typical of Miriam. When she thought she was not being understood, she just raised the volume of her voice. She didn't change her word choice the way some others do when they think they are being misunderstood. No, she just repeated the same phraseology, each time with greater fortitude and booming volume.

Taking advantage of the short lull in conversation, Melissa asked the rest of us how we were doing. Mercedes started to talk. She was dressed in a short skirt, leg warmers, and a cut-off sweatshirt. (It was the 1980s, after all.) She was all made up. Despite the fact that I certainly could not have worn the kind of outfit she sported, I couldn't help but notice that she was a beautiful woman.

Mercedes was a Marielito Cuban. In 1980, Fidel Castro opened his borders and allowed any Cuban who wanted to leave the country a free pass. Those who left departed from the port of Mariel, hence the term "Marielito Cuban." The U.S. Coast Guard, as well as some reservists turned active duty, were called in to assist the escaping Cubans. When all was said and done, about 125,000 Cubans were relocated to the United States. Most settled in Florida, where there was already a strong Cuban presence. As Mercedes shared with us, assimilation was not as easy as the refugees had expected.

"I am sorry to hear about your health. I hope you feel better soon," Mercedes said across the table to Miriam. "Thankfully, I am well, but I can't help thinking about my friends in Florida and how unwelcome they feel."

"What do you mean, Mercedes?" Melissa asked.

"Well, the whole world thinks we are just a band of crazies and criminals. It is hard to find work down there, and those of us who do speak English wind up more frustrated, because all we hear are the sneering comments made by others who think we can't understand them."

Mercedes paused to give the interpreters a chance to translate her comments. She then continued.

"People don't understand what we had to do to get out of Cuba! The government, as a condition of release, told us that we had to sign documentation indicating we were "deviant." I thought—we *all* thought—that this was just another bureaucratic technicality. We were always signing things here and there, and we did it because that is what you do in a communist country. Refusing to do what the government tells you to do is dangerous, if not deadly. Anyway, most of us *wanted* paperwork stating we were deviant because it allowed us to emigrate more easily! Then, when we came to the United States and the INS saw the paperwork, it got ugly. All over the news you would hear about how Castro had opened his mental hospitals and jails to the United States. Now, I know there were some among us who were less than honest or who were working with less than a full deck of cards. The vast majority of us, though, were good people looking for new opportunities. We only signed those documents so we could get out of the country!"

This time the interpreters asked Mercedes to pause while they tried to make sure they got the details of her story correctly translated.

Miriam interrupted, "Are you saying because you signed paper saying you 'deviant,' people are calling you criminal?"

"Yes!" Mercedes exclaimed.

"Damn communist," Miriam snarled to herself and anyone else who cared to listen.

"So, here I came to America, having been rescued by the U.S. Coast Guard, and all I faced was discrimination from those who thought I was either mental or crooked. Oh, and then some upper-class Cubans thought my entire cohort was uncultured and products of communist brainwashing. They were the most wealthy and well-educated Cubans, who left the country just after Castro came to power. The ones the revolution raged against on our behalf perhaps?" she added in a mocking tone.

"Anyway, there they sat on their manicured Florida lawns, judging their fellow countrymen. *Us!* It makes me so mad to even think about it. So, I decided to come to Michigan, where the controversy doesn't seem to be as bad. I had a few friends who had resettled up here, and they were largely content with their new lives. Basically I packed my bags and took a bus north."

"Have you had a warmer welcome in Greensburg?" Melissa asked.

"Yes, I definitely feel like the environment is less charged. I am sure people still have their thoughts about the Marielitos because there has been so much in the media. Even so, it is not *the* topic of conversation up here. People are more open-minded."

"And I am sure not *all* Floridians were judgmental of you folks, were they? I imagine that if you were to search your mind, you could identify several compassionate Cubans and Americans, couldn't you? There had to be a few people."

Melissa didn't do a lot of talking during our sessions, but at the same time she sought to strike a definite theme throughout our meetings. First, she always tried to steer us away from generalizing about groups of people. She wanted us to be able to vent our frustrations to one another, but she also wanted us to recognize that outright prejudice—something which we had all been the victims of ourselves—was not only a distortion of reality but ultimately unproductive. Perhaps, in her own way, she wanted to stop the circle of bitterness and hate. After all, we were refugees, and by definition the targets of generalizations, stereotypes, and blatant hatred. If we, sitting around this circle, then continued to contribute our own prejudices to the mix, nothing would ever change. Ultimately, Melissa was right, even though I was one of the people she had redirected on occasion.

"Mercedes—just tell us about a few who were kind and open-armed. Can you?" A sympathetic and encouraging smile broke across Melissa's face.

"Okay, yes. The soldiers, or whoever they were that picked us up, were kind to us, and I could tell they really wanted to make sure we reached shore safely. There was also an American grocer around the corner from me who, when I didn't have enough money for food, kept a tab for me until I could pay in full. We couldn't communicate all that well since he didn't speak Spanish and I struggled with English, but he was nice. He didn't have to do what he did."

"Kindness transcends language," one of the Hmong women said. She was one of the quietest of the group, but when she spoke she shared the most simple and yet inspiring thoughts. I *loved* that line: "Kindness transcends language." I decided to stow away the words—to put them somewhere for safekeeping.

"And the Cubans? Surely there were some redeeming people in the Cuban-American community? People who were not judgmental of you?" Melissa continued to try to bring Mercedes along.

"Hmmm, yes, there was this older couple who said they knew the media and the public had jumped on the story to our disadvantage. The wife offered to take me shopping for some clothes and have me over for a good Cuban dinner."

"Okay, good. I am glad you can think of some kind people while also remembering important parts of your own story in Florida."

After Miriam and Mercedes told us what was on their minds, it felt like the oxygen in the room had been depleted. Both were highly spirited women with strong views on the world and clear ideas about the way things should be. When they spoke, their words were punctuated by fluttering hands and flying tongues. By the time they were finished, their interpreters were as exhausted as they were.

Left in the room were the regulars: Aneesa who was Afghan, Shoua who was Hmong, and Nhu who was Vietnamese. Of course, there was me, but I wasn't interested in sharing anything that day.

Aneesa was also on the quiet side, but I did know she was a diplomat's wife who lost much when the Soviets invaded Afghanistan in 1979. The family was clearly wealthy, as Aneesa was always adorned in high-karat gold jewelry and wore crisp, tailored suits only found in the exclusive boutiques of Milan. She also had that air about her. She was not arrogant or snobby, but you could tell she had been places and had met important people in her lifetime. When we talked, her hands were always folded on her lap. The only time she ever moved was when she greeted someone "hello" or sipped her tea. She smiled when appropriate, but like me couldn't bring herself to say a great deal. I did know she and her husband had been in Europe when the Afghan government fell, so luckily their own lives had been spared. Of course, this is to say nothing of their extended family, whom she worried about but never directly spoke of.

Finally, there were Nhu and Shoua. I always had a hard time remembering their names because the sounds were so foreign to me. They were both lovely women whom I warmed up to right away. They were unassuming in their presence and so soft-spoken that their interpreters often asked them to repeat themselves. Shoua had remarked that "Kindness transcends language." Although I didn't know much about her, I listened closely when she spoke because her words always touched me or taught me something. The days her interpreter failed to show were a letdown. On those days in particular I wondered if she had any encouraging thoughts or bits of wisdom to offer us.

On that day at the Sewing Circle I had hoped we would hear more from Nhu and Shoua, but we only had an hour to talk, and the hour had passed.

"Well, we are about out of time this week, ladies. Thank you for coming, and I look forward to seeing you on Sunday," Melissa announced.

"Are we talking on Sunday?" Miriam asked in an anticipating voice.

"No, Sundays are just for sewing. We'll talk next Friday," Melissa replied.

"Ya, I like this talking business. My husband don't like hearing about my health," Miriam informed us.

I thought to myself, "Yeah, I *bet* he loves shipping you down here so he doesn't have to endure your daily medical monologue."

Soon after this thought entered my mind, I tried to correct myself. Again, Miriam was my elder, and I should respect her. Also, what did I gain by making myself even more frustrated by something insignificant? After all, far more important things were going on in my life, and surely, what I had lived through should have taught me to keep perspective.

So I gulped down a chilly mouthful of bitter tea and threw the cup into the garbage can. When it landed, it wasn't heavy enough to tip the top of the container. As it fell, little brown droplets of cold tea spread across the lid. As I shoved the cup down in, I thanked Melissa for the meeting and said my perfunctory good-bye to Aneesa, the diplomat's wife.

Outside, light snowflakes were zipping around city buildings. When I opened the heavy door, the frosty air washed across my face and felt refreshing. I tightened the scarf around my neck and pulled on my gloves, thinking about how I wanted to go home and at the same time did not. I felt overwhelmingly lonely and isolated, yet crowded and claustrophobic. I wanted to keep myself busy and occupied, but I also wanted to do nothing. I wanted to scream out in anguish for all the world to hear, but I wanted to seal my pain away in quiet forgetfulness. I wanted revenge, yet I wanted to forgive. I wanted to survive and triumph, while I wanted to give up and give in to the tragedies.

One contradiction after another filled my mind until, once on the bus, I closed my eyes and unclenched my fists. I focused on the hum of the engine and tried to block out all conversation around me. The latter was not that difficult since I barely understood what anyone was saying anyway.

In that moment, I didn't know how I would get through the next hour let alone the rest of my life. It was then I decided not to think about it all.

◆   ◆   ◆

Soon thereafter, while pushing my cart to the market, I stopped thinking about my wants, needs, desires, hopes, and regrets at all. All I thought about was what I should have to eat with my *badem-jan*, my eggplant.

Iran
Mid-Twentieth Century

When you come to the end of all the light you know, and it's time to step into the darkness of the unknown, faith is knowing that one of two things shall happen: Either you will be given something solid to stand on or you will be taught to fly.

Edward Teller

Chapter 4

My mother was a widow. My brother, sisters, and I were orphans. Why? Because this was mid-century Iran, a country that loved its men. Because, according to many, children who had no father might as well have no mother.

Looking back, I guess I had started to notice subtle changes in Baba. He would still smile at us when he came home from work and sneak us some candy, but he stopped boosting us up and over his shoulders and chasing us around the rose bushes. He used to tell us we were getting older now, but his face said something else. His once taut skin had started to sag, and his eyes, hair, and skin began to melt together into one shade of color. He also put in fewer hours at work, and he dressed in his house-clothes more often than in the fitted suits he had worn for as long as I had known him. His baggy pants ballooned into an even bigger size, and his dark blue shirt seemed to just hang on his pointed shoulders. I didn't like seeing Baba in his house-clothes, especially as he grew more sick. I longed to see him pull on his glossy trousers, fresh shirt, and his perfectly trimmed waistcoat. In fact, this vest was my most favorite part of his suit, because whenever I watched him fasten one button after another, stretch out his arms to uncrinkle his shirt, and clip his cufflinks, I believed my Dad was important. I was confident that he was about to embark on something meaningful.

Of course, I was only six years old when Baba died, so many of my memories are of him turning sick. He coughed so hard I was convinced he was tearing something deep inside himself. His long, celery stick legs bloated to double their size. He became weak to the point where Maman had to feed him, bathe him, and roll him from side to side on the bed so his skin would stay attached to his shrinking muscles. Had he been living today, here, he would have survived the heart condition that took his young life. Moreover, had he lived longer, I would have discovered what I had inherited from him and what I had not. After all, a prolonged relationship with someone allows you to see layers in that person. It allows you to see more deeply what he is made of, what your role in life relative to him is. None of these luxuries were open to me. My time with my father was pinched short.

◆   ◆   ◆

Shortly after our private moments around the koursey, an avalanche of people rolled into our home, tears and antics abounding.

"Oh my God, *this is so awful!* You must be devastated," one of my aunts said, as she pushed away her rolling tears and fanned herself with her handkerchief. "*Five* children to raise, *eh khoda!* My God! What will you do?"

"You should have something to eat. How about some fruit?" a cousin interrupted, pointing the head of a banana towards Maman's nose.

"No, she should have something more solid. How about some chicken?" another one said, lifting the lid on a pot to release wiggles of steam into the air.

"This is just so sad. I have such a headache," another aunt said, cupping her hands and tossing some pills into her dark, sparsely-toothed mouth.

"You should *blah-blah-blah ...* " said someone else.

"No, she should *blah-blah-blah ...* " added another. On and on people went. All their words sent Maman into an unblinking stare.

Until, that is, the boom and certitude of my uncle's voice cut through the chatter. "We'll take the children," he said, his declarative tone admitting no queries.

"*What?*" Maman said, blinking and lifting her eyes to his.

"You are tired and distracted right now. They should come with us. Children, get your things. We'll be leaving in a few minutes."

My stomach did a flip. I felt sick.

"Faheem, I can take care of them. I am fine, really." Maman said, still not moving her eyes from his.

"No, they should come with us. They are my brother's children."

As I listened to my mother and uncle talk, I watched my brother and sisters emerge with a travel bag stuffed with clothes they took no care in packing. In Irandokht's hand was her favorite, perfectly groomed doll, and in Khosro's was the model airplane he had just finished assembling the day before Baba died. All four of my siblings then walked their slumped bodies to the door, not wanting to go, but also afraid to defy our uncle.

I was still standing next to Maman.

"Come on, Meetra. Let's go, sweetheart," my aunt said, pulling on my hand. I didn't move easily. She took hold of my shoulders and started to guide me to the door. Afraid to cause trouble, I allowed my aunt to escort me across the room.

With every few steps I took away from Maman, I couldn't keep myself from glancing back.

My aunt began to help me with my jacket, stuffing my left arm, and then my right into the sleeves. Then she knelt down, buttoned the front, and rose. She stood behind me with her hands resting on my shoulders.

I remember tracing the lines of the red and blue geometric shapes on the carpet before lifting my head to look into the puddles in Maman's eyes. In that very same moment, she looked directly at me, and then at our uncle. "No!" she shouted. "*Please* don't take my children. *Don't take them from me!*"

With that, I stomped down as hard as I could on my aunt's toes. As my little foot crunched down on hers and she buckled forward in shock, I ran across the carpet and laced my arms around Maman's waist. I buried my teary, sweaty face in her soft belly, shut my eyes like a clam shell, and held on like a child who only had one parent left in the world.

Face buried, I listened to my aunt and uncle try and coax my mother into turning me over for a few days. Keeping her tight grip around me, Maman told our uncle how much she respected him and how well she understood established law regarding child custody issues. In the end, however, all I really remember is the patter of little feet followed by the sound of the front door slamming shut. Then, there was silence. There were still people in the room, but as they fanned themselves in nervousness and wonder they didn't say a word. When all was said and done, Maman may have released four of her children that night, but in a stunning act of fortitude and defiance, she had held onto at least one—the one tied around her waist.

◆   ◆   ◆

While Iranian tradition and culture handed a lot of power to the male relatives of a dead father, our baba did not. In an anachronistic move, Baba carefully drew up his will to insure that Maman would bear sole custody of us. Even more shocking, he specified that she would assume his position as partner in the textile business he shared with my uncle. The problem was that while Baba had full confidence in her ability to steer her way, society was not as conciliatory. No, Iran was not ready for a recently liberated and unveiled five-foot, one-hundred-pound woman to walk the passageways of the bazaar and negotiate business deals. And so, as determined as Maman was to stay at the helm, the reality was that she had to hire someone who would lend male legitimacy to our side of the shop. This meant any profits we would make would drop from fifty percent to twenty-five.

Baba's death affected us on many complex levels, but what we initially noticed were the obvious changes. First and foremost was the reality that our precious grandmother had to go.

Of all the women in our family, the stories of my grandmother are those told most frequently.

"She was a bone-setter," my mother used to tell us.

My grandmother was a tall, slender woman with long, curly, white hair. I only knew her hair was long because sometimes I would get a glimpse of it when she would comb it after her bath. I remember the comb slicing its way down her tresses and then getting stuck at a tangle maybe midway through. Then, once the comb had moved from end to end without interruption, she would weave the long pieces into a braid and pile it on top of her head.

She always wore a large, white, silk shawl that covered her from head to waist. She was a master silk weaver, and this was one of her many creations. She used to spend hours trying to teach me how to retrieve the thin silk filaments from cocoons and wind them by pulling and rolling them around wooden spindles. I remember watching the soft fluff turn to thread. I sat there, eyes squinting, waiting for the thread to break in two. It never did.

In addition to being such a skilled silk weaver, my grandmother was most famous for her bone-setting talents. Like her maternal ancestors before her, Beebee Jon had learned her craft from her mother's side of the family. She was one of the more famous healers in our parts, so week after week we would witness patient after patient rapping on the door for a consultation. My grandmother would appear, shawl in place, and take the distressed patient in for an exam. If the patient's injury was too severe, she would refer him to the hospital. If, on the other hand, she was able to care for him, she would use the skeleton that literally hung in her closet to explain her diagnosis.

One day as Khosro and I were chasing each other in the yard, Grandmother called out and motioned us to come to her workshop. The patient before us was a young boy who had fallen out of a tree and could not straighten his arm. Right there, without words, Beebee Jon jetted her eyes our way to let us know she would be none too pleased to see us playing in high and dangerous places. From there, she quietly but confidently ran her fingers along the boy's arm and, as he flinched in pain, uttered some words of comfort.

Once she completed her exam, she curled her long, arthritic finger our way and escorted us to the hanging skeleton in her closet. As she opened the door, he swayed and then settled. Beebee Jon then pointed to his forearm, wrist bone, and the eight small bones on his hand. She then started to show us which bone on the young boy's arm was broken. As she lectured on, all I could think about was how my grandmother had gotten a skeleton in her workshop? Who was he? In life, did he ever think that in death he would be hanging from a piece of string tied to a thick nail?

Unlike me, Khosro listened attentively to Beebee. He soon took his own fingers and ran them along the length of the skeleton's arm. He paused in places where there were connections, and Beebee Jon said, "Joint."

With no help from me, Grandmother and Khosro decided the boy had broken his forearm and needed a cast. At this point, Beebee reached for the flour and eggs. All I could think of was, "Cake!"

"No," said Beebee Jon. "This will eventually harden to the point where the boy will not be able to move his arm. It will allow the bone to heal."

Still on the sidelines, I watched the two mix a cup of this and a handful of that until the mixture was right. Then they soaked the bandages in the concoction and layered the cloths along the boy's arm. Once the cast hardened, the boy left with instructions to return in a few weeks for its removal.

Obviously no medical prodigy, I do have to say I was most taken by Beebee's ability to handle a water pipe. Each week, as she closed shop and prepared for her day off, I would watch her loosen her braid from her head, search the kitchen for a hot cup of tea and some sweet dates, and lift the ornate water pipe from the shelf before falling back into her favorite cushioned chair. Beebee's pipe was tall and looked something like an elongated genie bottle. It had a sky-blue glass base painted with delicate flowers. A brass pipe extended up from the base, and a smoking tube jetted out from its side. Beebee was always conscientious about making sure her charcoal and tobacco were ready for her long-awaited and—from her perspective—well-deserved Thursday night ritual.

As she sat there, relishing her vice, Maman's presence in the house magnified. We could hear her banging her feet onto the floor as she walked. When she went from one room to another, she would make sure the door shut firmly. She blustered through the rooms she was tidying, darting by while Beebee kept her eyes closed and her head rested on the back of the chair. Sometimes I even heard her humming a tune as she let the tobacco smoke fill her lungs. Without interruption or regard for the chill in the air, she kept sucking. She was her own woman.

◆   ◆   ◆

Custom dictates that a mother must live with her eldest son, so now that Baba was gone Beebee Jon had to go too. She only moved to my uncle's house, but it felt much farther away than that. Perhaps it was also what her leaving symbolized. It was as though we were no longer worthy of her. It was as though Baba had secured a certain station for us, and now that he was gone, we had fallen to another layer. This was the first time I realized that others didn't necessarily see us as a "real" family any more—at least not one as real as my uncle's. In my uncle's family, there was a Maman and a Baba.

From a financial standpoint, Beebee's leaving was probably a wise move. After all, with Maman having to hire a man to represent her in the business, our family income had dropped by fifty percent. That said, emotionally it hurt. As I watched Beebee stuff her shawls into her suitcase and brush away the tears she thought she was hiding from me, I felt shame for the first time in my life. I felt as though we were unworthy of Beebee and therefore somehow illegitimate. I didn't know, however, that this feeling would become all too familiar as I grew up and started to make my way into the world.

Accompanying the stigma and sadness of having lost Beebee Jon, Maman soon realized that our servants Badree and Ali had to go too. They had lived with us for years and had helped Maman and Baba with various jobs around the house. They were like family to us, but now that we were unable to pay their salaries, we said good-bye to them as well.

Next, we turned our house into a business opportunity by renting out our extra rooms. All six of us piled into one room that had to serve all our needs. What I remember most were the nights. Even when we wanted to turn in at different times, because we all slept in the same space we were coaxed into falling into a common schedule. So, once bedtime struck, we would pull out our "beds"—bundles of sheets and blankets really—and roll them out across the floor. Covering this same floor, hours before, had been a tablecloth upon which our evening meal had been laid out. It was the same floor, framed by the same walls, we had just studied on too.

Needless to say, what once felt like a big slumber party turned into a claustrophobia-inducing cell. I had no private space to myself, and there were times I feared my brother and sisters could see my dreams. Our heads almost touched one another as we slept, and I was convinced that my latest crush and other even more private thoughts could somehow be seized by the brain so close to mine. As if that were not enough, on restless nights I was guaranteed to find someone's head, fingers, toes, on my blanket or—one night in particular—up my nose!

That night, Khosro was in a devilish mood. Once I had fallen asleep and Maman had stepped out of the room for a minute, Khosro stuck his fingers up my nose while I rested in sweet slumber. Shocked awake, all I could do was slap his mischievous hand as his guilty fingers left my sleeping quarters and entered his.

◆   ◆   ◆

In the weeks and months following Baba's death, we all dealt with our loss differently. Maman was private for the most part, crying when she thought no one else could see or hear her. She also scurried around the house even faster than she used to, finding chores for all of us to work on. As for my two oldest sisters, they created their own cocoon in which they shared their secrets and fears. I never really remember talking to them about Baba.

Irandokht? She prayed. She prayed morning, noon, and night. Sometimes she would read, but then I would catch her praying again. I remember her saying, *"Khoda bozorg ast,"* God is all powerful. I felt angry that she trusted fate to lead us where we needed to be.

As for me, I couldn't sleep because I knew that Baba had died while sleeping. I somehow connected the two and sought to avoid both. I'd lay there night after night listening to my brother and sisters snore and wonder where Baba was and whether if I too were to die I would join him. Briefly comforted by the thought of being with him again, I then thought of Maman and how I couldn't bear to be separated from her.

Dilemmas and questions, both practical and spiritual, filled my mind. Where was Baba's body? Could he see everything I did throughout the day? Was he watching me and my every move?

My most potent memory of this time was of a bird. One day I was sitting in our room reading quietly when a sparrow in full flight hit the windowpane. When I hurried outside to see if it was all right, I saw it lying on the ground, neck bent. *Contorted.* I didn't have the heart to tell anyone about the incident. I left it lying there in the grass. Within a few days, its body bloated up, and creatures started to feast on its corpse. I remember thinking of Baba and wondering, hoping, he was safe from scavengers.

As for Khosro, I rarely saw him cry. I do, however, remember him stretching his hand across his forehead and complaining about headaches. And then, there were more than a few times he ran out of the house, just about to lose his dinner over an upset stomach. He also got into several fights at school. They were scuffles really. It usually started when someone made fun of him for being an orphan and he retorted, informing them otherwise. More than once, he followed up his declarations with a forceful shove, and from there it escalated.

The only time I ever saw Khosro cry was on a nondescript day as we were walking home from school. As we wound our way down the narrow streets, we chatted about what had happened that day and mocked our teachers. Suddenly, we were stopped by some street children, probably the same ones we had passed tens of times on our way to and from school that year. Sadly, the Tehran streets were home to many children who had no other place to live. Each day as we ambled along, there they would be, invisible to those of us who had gotten used to seeing them.

On this particular day, as was typical, one of the young boys approached us and asked us for some money and food. We would usually decline, keep walking, and not think much more of the encounter. This day, however, was different. At least for Khosro. As the young boy came toward us, Khosro stopped walking. He watched the boy approach, and as the child's odor filled the air around us, Khosro looked coldly into the boy's green eyes. The child had patches of dirt on his face, but streaks of white skin lined his cheeks. I guessed that fresh tears had just carved their way down through the soil. His hair was matted and dusty, his fingernails filled with grime. His body was covered in torn clothes, and his hands were dotted with scabs—remnants of what he had done to survive on the streets that week.

"Please, sir, *dah-shahee?*" Ten pennies? "*Dah-shahee?* Or some *nan?*" We had been taught never to give to beggars who stopped us on the street, and so we had never before indulged them.

I yanked on Khosro's sleeve and motioned for us to start walking, but Khosro didn't move.

"Please, sir, have mercy," the boy said, getting down on his knees and cupping his hands. As he looked up at Khosro, hoping for leniency, Khosro shuffled his nervous feet and suddenly shifted in such a way so as to inadvertently cause the sunlight to blast over his shoulder and into the child's eyes. The intense rays forced the boy to bow his head. Forsaken, there he knelt, head down, hands open, and shaking.

With that, tears poured down Khosro's face, and his own hands started to shake too. He rummaged through his bookbag for loose change. In a gruff voice, he instructed me to do the same. As he dug through his bag, his stream of tears turned into a surge. Soon, his busy hands became distracted by his runny nose, and he threw his bag on the ground, knelt down, and used one hand to dig and the other to dry his wet face. Passersby started to slow their walk as they came by. Some even pointed at us and mumbled to their companions.

After thoroughly searching our bags, we could only come up with a half a piece of bread between us. Spines curved, heads slumped, we handed the boy the bread and started back to the house. As I turned around one last time to look at the child, I saw that he had scampered into the corner of an abandoned building. With breakneck speed he was devouring the *nan*. His teeth couldn't work fast enough to feed his starved body.

When we came through the heavy door of our home, Khosro raced his eyes from one end of the room to the other in search of Maman. As soon as he spotted her by the window, he threw his bag down on the floor, ran to her, and wrapped his arms around her waist. Surprised and unprepared for the force by which he came at her, Maman took a slight step backwards to brace herself as she embraced him.

I could see that Maman was almost about to scold him for not taking off his shoes—until she saw his face. She folded her arms around him and turned to me, eyebrows elevated and head tilted in question. While she rubbed his back to comfort him, I told her it all started when Khosro saw the street children—the orphans who had first lost their baba and then found they had no maman to take care of them either.

Maman never said a word to us. She just held us close. There were no guarantees in this life. She knew it, and we were just beginning to know it ourselves.

Chapter 5

As the years drew farther away from Baba's death, we found ourselves growing and creating a life separate from the one we had known. Psychologically, we had been raised to believe that Baba would be the one to pull us back from trouble. He always had done just that. Early in my parents' marriage, he had rebuilt our family fortune after thieves walked away with all the money he had earned. A slip of sweet poison to our watchdogs and *wham*! Out of the house walked all our gold, silver, and savings. Thanks to Baba's hard work, however, we rejoined the middle class a few years later. Then, when the Shah of Iran wanted to expand his military and needed our property to do it, Baba saved us a second time. Within days of being evicted from our house, our father secured another home for us. It became the only home I would ever know while growing up.

Now, with Baba gone, it took time for Maman to settle into her new role as head of the household. Once grown, I discovered she had been approached about remarriage by suitors who were interested in taking her as a wife. Maman always declined, however, and until the day she died she never had another romantic relationship. Like a lot of widows, she was more afraid of marrying someone who would be ill-suited for her children than she was about being alone. She knew marriage would dilute her influence over her family, and in the worst case, bring her children added pressures and worries that she could neither control nor thwart. My mother was thirty-five when Baba died, although as a child she seemed "old" to me. Once I reached my mid-thirties, however, I realized how young she really was to make such permanent, personal sacrifices for us.

◆   ◆   ◆

As Maman stayed vigilant about protecting us and raising us into adulthood, we continued to live out our childhoods. Irandokht spent most of her life either in the kitchen or in one sort of book or another. Maman, believing words were only tools to let someone know what to do or what mistakes they had made, didn't say much to Irandokht. There were many times, however, I would catch her kissing my sister on the cheek or patting her shoulder in gratitude. No words—just a gesture. That was Maman. No need to waste air on the obvious.

As for Khosro and Aram, they turned their attention away from the game of *Zeshteh-ya-Mahe* and went into the moviemaking business. They made their projector out of a wooden box connected to two-hundred-and-twenty volts of electricity. Then, they placed a mirror behind a light and ran a thirty-five-millimeter filmstrip through a channel. Their invention also had a magnifying glass and something resembling a telescope that helped focus the picture.

Each week, they rummaged through discarded film the local movie theaters had thrown out. They scraped off the film, and with Irandokht's help drew their own stories on the strip. Special features included scenes from *Ali Baba and the Forty Thieves* and the classic Persian tales of Shireen and Farhad. They named their makeshift movie theater "Aram-Kho"—obviously a play on their own names, but also a word meaning "calmness" in Persian. They hoped that those who entered the movies that afternoon would find a break, a respite, from the world outside.

While Maman surely liked Khosro's more productive endeavors, she was forever screaming, "You kids are going to electrocute yourselves!" I still remember that wooden spoon shaking at the two of them.

During this same time, I was growing and learning about myself too. I so wanted to be like Irandokht and help Maman. Even though Maman said very little in the way of praise, I knew Irandokht was the kind of daughter who made her exhale. If Khosro made her inhale, it was Irandokht who definitely let her get the air out of her pent-up lungs. I did an okay job, but I was no Irandokht, and I think some of this had to do with the fact that Maman thought I focused on the frivolous. While she was worrying about how we were going to survive, I was engaging her in idle conversation about dress patterns, colors, and questions about which earrings better matched my outfit. I don't know why this was such a dilemma. After all, I didn't have that many clothes to choose from anyway.

But then, just when Maman thought I was turning shallow, my other self would show, and her eyes would compress in smile. When I would tell her about how I had stood up for those in trouble, Maman always put her spoon down and looked me in the eye until I was finished. Then, she would flash a grin so wide that I could see her back teeth. Her favorite stories were of times I would make every effort to protect the innocent, whether this meant informing my teachers of bullies or yanking on Khosro's sleeve and making the two us walk home with a child whom we knew would be teased once outside school grounds. Maman was a fighter, and she expected the same courage from us. While Irandokht was the most principled of us—she knew right and did right—I was probably the most justice-oriented. My mother told me she saw glimpses of this trait in me as far back as the age of two. Apparently, though I was a helpless toddler myself at the time, when I would see another child in distress I would yell "Help!" at the top of my lungs. My wobbly legs may have only stood inches from the ground, but when I steadied them, clenched my fists, and screamed for assistance, the adults came running.

Maman secretly hoped my baby outrage was a peek into the kind of adult, the kind of woman, I would become. I hoped so too, but life has a way of turning out differently than we plan.

Chapter 6

Every family needs a crazy aunt. We sure had one, and we called her Khaleh, which means, quite simply, "aunt." We had several khalehs in our life, but whenever we failed to attach an identifying name to the term—Khaleh Soraya or Khaleh Leila—we all knew exactly who we were talking about.

Khaleh, Maman's great aunt actually, always showed up unannounced and uninvited. When she arrived, however, the winds shifted course.

We would always hear her before we saw her. As she made her way down the street, she would shout a robust "Hello!" and "How are you!" to anyone she could reach. She didn't know those she greeted, but she greeted them nonetheless. She also loved to sing, so when there was no one on the street to bombard, she trumpeted tunes.

Like Maman, she had curly, frizzy hair. Unlike Maman, the hair was the first thing you noticed about Khaleh when you finally did see her. It was as though a bird had landed on the top of her head and set up house. Pieces went east and west and, in some strange way, wound up circling around into something loosely resembling a nest.

Then there were the outfits. Again, Iran was a conservative country during my childhood, and while my family did not veil, modesty and a conservative color scheme was a must. On top of that, Maman was fanatic when it came to cleanliness. Some of it had to do with trying to get ahead of the latest virus circling the neighborhood, and some of it had to do with simple pride. My maman, for example, whether planning to stay home or go out, always looked neat, put together, and on a good day quite lovely.

Khaleh, on the other hand, wore shapeless clothes too big for her rotund frame. She also wore colors that tended to be awfully loud for our part of the world. Not only that, they were mismatched. Stripes folded into dots and tassels tied on for ornamentation were all common when it came to Khaleh's attire. Finally, her shoes were always untied. Interestingly enough, that never slowed her down as she angled the corner and bounded into the house.

Her knock on our front door always followed her entry into the hallway. This sudden entry never really mattered anyway though, because we always heard her coming before we saw her.

In she came, hair-nest minus the bird, and shoelaces going every which way. When Khosro, Irandokht, and I saw her, we all steadied our legs and turned wooden. This was of no concern to Khaleh, who darted across the room, engulfed us in her fat arms, and plunked one kiss after another on us. Then she took our soon-to-be-numb cheeks and pinched them between her thumb and index finger. Back and forth she would swing our heads, our little faces in her finger-vise.

"Oh, my babies, how are you? You're so cute. So beautiful! What are you up to these days? Why don't you come and see me?" Kiss, kiss, kiss....

"Khaleh ..." Khosro started to interrupt.

"Oh, my boy, I love you so much. My, have you grown. And Irandokht, what a lady you have become. I love you all so much. Meetra, my goodness, I think about you all the time. My little one ... I love you. Why don't you come to visit me? I am alone. You should come see me. I am your Khaleh!"

By this point in the "conversation," as was the case every time, Maman emerged and shepherded Khaleh out of the room. We stood there, rubbing our red cheeks and shaking our heads, until the two reemerged, Khaleh with a fistful of cash and Maman exasperated.

As Khaleh would float out the door and back down the street, we would all look at Maman for sympathy. Using the palms of her hands to push back the pieces of her hair that always came loose in stressful times, she would say, "She is family."

Nothing more was ever said of Khaleh.

◆   ◆   ◆

"Come and get it, fresh milk!" I heard the old man yell. I tore into the house and got our storage containers. Once back on the street, I was soon joined by all my neighbors who were also vying for the latest supply of fresh milk. The milk-man, now older, was the same one I had known all my life. As he slowed, I caught sight of the wire baskets on the side of his bicycle. Each of us offered up our bottles, and he ladled the milk into them. The later it got in the day, the lower the spoon would sink into his canister. By early evening, it clanked along the sides as he fetched the last cups of milk for us. No matter the weather, the old man rounded the neighborhood in search of customers. Like the rest of us, he knew his family only ate as well as his ability to work his body into sunset and beyond.

This was mid-twentieth century Tehran—at least the Tehran I knew. What I didn't know at the time, however, was that this seemingly obscure activity, buying milk, was a privilege not necessarily available to the rest of my country's people.

How did I come to know this? Because of my short, absurd stay in Tuyserkan.

It started with my oldest sister's marriage, which bumped Khosro from his position as male head-of-household. My brother-in-law, now in the lead, decided we should all move to Tuyserkan. He had been asked to bring a modern water supply system to the area, so up and out we all went, modern plumbing in mind.

Maman wasn't too keen on leaving Tehran, but with young children to raise and little money, she reluctantly agreed. Khosro and I rolled our eyes, threw our hands up in protest, but it didn't matter. Irandokht said nothing.

While Tuyserkan was not that far away from us geographically, it was a world away culturally. Certainly, relative to western cities, Tehran still had a way to go. According to Iranian standards, however, it was a thriving and modern city compared to many of the nation's outlying areas.

◆　　　◆　　　◆

On my first day in Tuyserkan, I downed a full glass of water and two cups of tea.

"Where is the bathroom?" I asked my brother-in-law.

"There is no bathroom. Over there you will find a hole in the ground," he said. He kept his head down and shuffled some papers into a loose pile. Sweat was sliding down the side of his face, and the humidity had turned the few pieces of hair on his head into short fuzz.

"*A hole!*" I shrieked.

Head still down, he pulled out another batch of papers, licked his finger, and started to thumb through them. Head drooped and hands in my pockets, I made my way to the hole.

As I crossed a stretch of grass that was broken up by dusty patches of dead vegetation, I went behind the only bush I could see. Off to the side, shrouded by a makeshift wooden structure, I found the hole. As I looked down at the black, smelly, cavity, the only word that came to me was "*Poof!*" Yes, one botched move and in I would go, swallowed up by the crater and its contents.

I proceeded to drink very little in Tuyserkan.

◆   ◆   ◆

It soon came time for the next generation of our family to be born. My sister had been expecting for months. When dagger-like pains stretched their way across her abdomen, we went in search of help. There were no nurses or doctors in the area, but there was an old woman with "experience." When it came time, Khosro ran to her clay hut and brought her back to us. She was dressed in a faded black, dirty chador that she unsuccessfully tried to keep wrapped around her bony body. When she smiled, her pink gums broke through her chapped lips. She had no teeth.

"I have delivered hundreds of babies. I could do it asleep," she said as she tottered in, wheezing for breath.

Since I wasn't the one having a baby, it seemed like the old woman had no sooner arrived than I heard an infant scream in the other room. A toothless smile and a pair of shaking hands appeared from behind the dirty pink curtain. Before my brother-in-law could get a tear down his cheek, she plopped the child into his arms and was three feet out the door. As she meandered away, tilted over and clutching her lower back, her chador dragged on the ground behind her. I heard her let out a grunt and then a moan. Clearly, she had been less than awestruck by the "miracle" of birth.

I, personally, couldn't wait to hold my new nephew. As I elbowed Irandokht aside, I caught a glimpse of my other sister's face. It was covered in an ugly rash that sand-flies had brought to her. *Salak*—oriental sores—they called it. She looked angry without even trying, and as I looked at Maman, making sure not to drop the baby, I could see she was about as bewildered as the old lady had looked.

After two years' time, efforts to bring a modern water supply to Tuyserkan presented more challenges then results. Maman was the quickest to see the futility of the project. With a simple, "*Bereem*! Let's go!" she slapped one last sand-fly dead, packed our bags, and took us back to Tehran.

Our expectations about what Tehran could offer us upon return turned out to be inflated. Tuyserkan had caused us to romanticize our capital city, and it wasn't too long before we realized that we were still poor and—in the eyes of society—a Baba-less, fractured family.

As I grew and matured, so many competing thoughts flooded my mind. I knew I wanted to stay close to Maman and protect her, but I also wanted to escape and strike out on my own. I wanted to hold tight to our precious family, preserve traditions, and keep Baba's memory alive. I also wanted to bolt. I wanted to forget the past and shed the labels society had branded us with. I didn't want to be an "orphan," "fatherless," "poor," and worst of all, "inadequate." I wanted *new* labels, which meant separating myself from Maman. This was a thought I couldn't bear, however.

I started to realize that my childhood had taught me how tenuous life is. How in a flicker of an instant life can change. For forever.

Some nights, sleep didn't come easy. I worried Maman would die too, I worried about how she would keep us afloat, and I worried about what would happen next to change our lives.

Bad nights turned these worries into obsessions, and I started to realize that no matter how much I tried to appear as strong as Maman, secretly I was hunkered down, waiting, expecting something bad to happen. I believed life could slam me at any moment with some new, shocking revelation that would change the rhythm I knew and counted on. I feared the jolt; I feared the fallout.

Others saw me as light-hearted and resilient, but these were my private thoughts—my never-uttered fears.

Greensburg, Michigan
The 1980s

The only tyrant I accept in this world is the still voice within.

Mahatma Gandhi

Chapter 7

The week had spun around to Friday again, which meant it was my day to head to Second Chances. I hadn't been there in a few weeks, because I had recently started a housekeeping job at a local hotel. Had my language skills been better, I could have worked elsewhere. Still limping along in broken English, I found myself in a job cleaning rooms most days.

As I headed out the door for the bus stop, I took a listen for my fiery neighbor and his tortured child. I had not heard them in a while and secretly hoped the father had moved on and left his son in safekeeping. It took me a long time to move the image of that child into the periphery of my mind. I prayed his toss into the back seat was the greatest wound inflicted on him that day, but my gut told me otherwise.

Since becoming a mother, I have forever seen my son's face in any suffering. Every hungry, hurt, and abandoned child bears my son's likeness. To see a child in pain is to see my own son in anguish. Perhaps this is the burden and the humanity motherhood delivers us.

◆　　　◆　　　◆

So I left the apartment and loaded onto the first of two buses that would take me to Second Chances. As I slid into the seat, I could feel my bones shifting to get comfortable. Working against them were my sore muscles, which hoped I would rest them for just a few minutes. My hands were a deep pink color, and they burned. They were casualties of the hot bedsheets I had pulled out of the industrial dryer the day before.

My job was physical—extremely physical. I stripped and remade soiled beds, carried loads of laundry, and cleaned bathrooms. That part of the job was the worst: most people took little care to clean up after themselves when they knew someone else would do it. Bundles of used tissues filled the counter and the floor around the trash can. Hair filled the tub, and when the toilet overflowed it was left for me to discover and address.

All that aside, the hardest aspect of the job was how some people treated me. Most just looked past me, not seeing me at all, but others—usually a guests—would ask me a question too quickly or in an accent I couldn't understand. Some used vocabulary I hadn't yet learned or talked to me while eating, lighting a cigarette, or mumbling. If I asked them to repeat themselves so I could decipher what they were saying, my puzzled face brought about the retort, "*Damn immigrant!*" Even more insulting, I actually think there were people who thought I didn't want to learn English, which was the most outrageous part of the whole encounter.

I felt like screaming, "*Not* learn English? Are you *crazy*? Do you think I *like* not understanding what people are saying? Do you think I *like* going to the grocery store and spending hours there because I can't make out what the products are? Do you think I feel at all intelligent having to look at the *pictures* on cans of food to determine their contents? What about going to the doctor's office when I am sick and not being able to tell the doctor what's wrong with me? Or getting a prescription and not understanding the directions on the medicine vial? How do you think people look at me then? Do you think that I actually *like* being treated like I am stupid? How about being called a damn immigrant?"

Who the *hell* would come to this country and not want to learn English?

Oh, and by the way, how long do you think it actually takes to learn a language? I'll answer that for you—*years*! Probably longer than that! Didn't you study a foreign language in high school? How many years did you study? And you're fluent in that language now, right?

So, if you don't mind, *monolingual* person that you are, can you please slow down a little bit and repeat what you said? I am learning more each day, and I thank you in advance for your patience!"

I do have a winged tongue—it just flies a lot faster in Persian.

◆   ◆   ◆

So, work was work. It helped me pay the bills, and at minimum wage each penny was carefully allocated. I decided to stop buying meat and replace my protein needs with beans. Pound for pound, the savings was incredible. I also decided to try and use canned vegetables instead of fresh ones. That was a much harder sacrifice. I made all my own bread, often thinking of the *nan*-maker of my youth. Of course, I used rice as a staple with every meal. I never bought juice or other beverages. The house only had the water from the spigot and the tea I couldn't help but buy. Despite my love of tea, I did train myself to curtail my drinking to only those times when I was entertaining company. This stretched the box far longer. Oh yes, I bought loose tea rather than the bags. It traveled further.

Of course, there were also lights to shut off. My rule was this: only one light on at a time in the apartment. I had to think of many ways to trim my costs. Each month I was faced with regular payments to my landlord, the utility company, the transportation authority, and the airline that brought me to America. My ticket to the United States had been prepaid, but I was required to reimburse the organization that had put up the money. The bill was several thousand dollars. When all was said and done, by the end of the month I just plain ran out of money.

Yes, life had changed dramatically. I was shocked when I paused to think about it. I was poor, very poor, and yet—ironically—I was in America. As newcomers, refugees, we all seem to have something in common. We arrive thinking the gates will open when we step through Customs. We hope that suddenly all the hardship we endured on our way here will be replaced with economic security and easier days. Don't get me wrong—life in Greensburg was certainly better than where I came from. Although I lived in what Americans called a "bad" neighborhood, and I feared being the victim of a random crime, I was absolutely safer in most respects.

I guess when you escape from a country, you pin your hopes on an unrealistic notion of what you will come into when you finally break away. You dream so you can find the motivation and courage to leave.

Chapter 8

As I pushed open the heavy green door to Second Chances, I could hear the chatter in the sewing room. Russian, Vietnamese, Spanish, and other languages were crowding the air as I lugged my tired body down the stairs.

Once in the room, I was welcomed by kind faces and lots of smiles. Funny. I would not have thought people even remembered me, let alone recognized my return. I scanned the room for Aneesa, the woman from Afghanistan, the diplomat's wife. Drowning in English day and night, I couldn't wait to talk with someone in my own language. Someone with whom I could let my tongue fly.

"Where is Aneesa?" I asked Melissa.

"She moved to California …" The rest of what Melissa said escaped me. Yet another line of English sounds.

I did catch that Aneesa had left, however. When I heard the news, my stomach dropped in disappointment. At the same time, I wasn't surprised. There was a large Afghan community in California, and some even said it was like a "little Kabul." A lot of the established families knew one another. I imagined that adjusting was a little bit easier. I didn't blame Aneesa for going, but I did feel a bit jealous.

I started to look around the room for other women I knew and spotted Mercedes, who flashed a huge smile and an "*Hola*!" my way. Then I saw Miriam, who was fanning herself and clutching her back.

Not wanting to catch her eye, I looked at the clock and then noticed the women packing up their fabric. It was time to talk. As Melissa reached for the Lipton tea box and some brownies she had made, I pulled out a chair beside Nhu and Shoua and sat down. Miriam fell into a seat across from me, and Aneesa's regular spot was empty.

Instead of going around and asking each one of us how we were doing that week, Melissa offered up a general "hello" and "welcome." She then introduced us to a new woman from the USSR who, like Miriam, was a Jewish refugee. This woman was younger, however, and had lived in Israel before coming to the United States. She told us she wasn't particularly religious and consequently felt more at ease in the United States than she had in Israel. Miriam exhaled particularly loudly when she heard this. Then, the other new refugees introduced themselves. Miriam, about whose well-being Melissa did not ask directly, huffed and puffed. You could see she was on the verge of becoming unplugged. She could not *wait* to be asked about her life and health. Melissa never looked at her.

"Shoua and Nhu, how are you ladies today?"

As Melissa leaned in towards them, looked them in the eyes, and smiled with warmth, she made *me* want to participate for a moment. Shoua and Nhu then looked down at their hands and jerked their heads forward in a way that suggested they were fine.

While Shoua and Nhu had different experiences from one another, in many ways they were both casualties of U.S. foreign policy in Vietnam. Shoua was Hmong and from Laos. From what I understand, in addition to Vietnam, the United States was also fighting communist forces in Laos. The short of it was that many of the Hmong in Laos were helping the United States, and so, when the Communists won, the Americans felt obligated to help the Hmong who had stood by them.

Somehow, Shoua and her family had made it to the United States, and Greensburg specifically. She was the woman who uttered those simple words: "Kindness transcends language." She had led me to believe that, while I did not know her personal story, I knew what *type* of person she was. Funny how it's often the quiet ones who reveal so much.

In that vein, unlike Miriam, Shoua was not interested in being understood, sympathized with, or known. She needed no witness to her life. She came to the Sewing Circle to sew, and she talked because that is what we did afterwards. While I was profoundly curious about Shoua, drawn to her in some strange way, I could obviously relate to her desire to keep her life private—her need to keep her secrets hidden. After all, I had come to the Sewing Circle for weeks and never offered up anything other than polite responses. By now, even Melissa had learned to respect my muted tongue.

Realizing that Shoua was not interested in sharing any further, Melissa turned to Nhu. Nhu was from Vietnam, and her husband had been a university professor in the south. Apparently, he was also a U.S. sympathizer, which caught up with him when the country fell to the communists.

In previous conversations, Nhu had told us she had had a good life in Vietnam. She had had a large home she loved and help around the house. Both faculty and students had respected and cared for her husband. Like many of us, she had trusted and counted on the security she found herself in.

The war then started, and as the years progressed, life changed. In what seemed like a flash, the Americans pulled out, her husband lost his job, and he was ordered to report to a reeducation camp. These camps, established by the communists after 1975, imprisoned people from the southern armed forces, religious leaders, intellectuals, American employees, officials of the former government, and anyone else deemed a threat to the regime.

"Campers," as they called prisoners, were told to pack enough to sustain themselves for ten days. Most were held for years. In these camps, victims were forced to do hard labor and told to "reform their thoughts." Little food was available and virtually no health care. In a cruel act of torture, prisoners were often asked to betray other prisoners as a condition of release. Their fellow inmates, whom they had grown attached to over the years, were now bargaining chips in the game of survival.

Before her husband had been sent to the reeducation camp, Nhu worried deeply about the fate of her young family. She had two infant daughters, and in a desperate moment of panic, she had considered sending them to America with the thousands of other babies who were being airlifted from the region. Technically, only orphans were being evacuated, but Nhu had heard that some parents were offering their children up as orphans in order to save their lives. Some of these parents planned on reuniting with their children in America; others simply let theirs go. They took a leap of faith, convincing themselves that "life on the other side" would be kinder.

Nhu talked to her husband about "Operation Baby Lift"—what this project was ultimately called—but he would hear nothing of it. He said that she was overreacting to the pending communist threat, and that everything would be okay.

Soon thereafter, he was sent to a reeducation camp. She felt widowed. He was ultimately released, and—long story short—they escaped from Vietnam to a refugee camp. They had heard that many refugees had been turned away in Malaysia. In fact, if a boat were to even *make* it to Malaysia—a feat in its own right, as most boats were overcrowded, leaky, and lacking any kind of navigation equipment—refugees were ambushed once they got there. They heard horrific stories of refugees being raped, kidnapped, and murdered by bandits. As if that were not enough, stories emerged about how Malaysia had actually towed back out to sea boats that were chock full of refugees and shot them point blank.

Apparently, the best camps were in Hong Kong, while the worst were in Thailand. I never caught where Nhu and her family wound up, but I do know she lost her daughters along the way. By then they were toddlers, but as any mother knows, even with a couple of years under their belts toddlers are every bit as vulnerable as infants.

Nhu never shared these details with us herself. I learned Nhu's story through her interpreter. To be sure, the translator broke confidence when she told us these wrenching details, but I think, in the end, she just needed to lift the horror of the story from her own shoulders.

Although I didn't realize it at the time, interpreters have a difficult role to play in this dance. They are the first to hear us speak, and they are the ones who must give words, voice, to our thoughts. At times, the glass barrier between one person and another fogs up. At times, empathy takes over and emotions blend. In those moments, the interpreter feels what the client feels. She lives the story and finds the words that give it a second life.

◆　　　◆　　　◆

Realizing Shoua was finished offering her input for the day, Melissa turned to Nhu. "How is your husband's job?" she asked.

"It is hard. He gets very tired, and he always smells like spoiled food when he comes home. His hands are often burnt, and he says it hurts to turn the pages of his book. He is not happy. He misses his students."

Nhu's husband, the professor, was now working at a local banquet hall as a dishwasher. For hours he would load and empty the machine, thinking all the while about his books, his students, and his fractured family. He only had one novel he could read, the one he had brought with him from Vietnam. Although he was surrounded by books he could easily check out of the library, he could read none of them until he learned English. How sad—an intellectual cut off from the world of ideas. A doctor turned dishwasher.

Melissa continued to draw Nhu out, asking her about her own job search. Nhu shook her head, telling us that while she and her husband needed money, he was the traditional type and thus resistant to her working. He had always been the one to support their family. Although their circumstances had obviously changed, Nhu's husband's cultural beliefs were far slower to catch up to these changes.

Nhu herself wanted to work, as she knew one salary between them was not enough. More importantly, however, she told us that idle time at home just made her cry. She hoped that being busy, working, would stem the rush of tears she couldn't halt on her own. Though she knew she would never get rid of her tears, she hoped that work might keep them at bay, if only until evening. Melissa asked her what she cried about.

"My babies," she said.

"My babies … my babies … my babies … my babies." The refrain sounded in my mind over and over. The interpreter had only said it once, but I heard the words echo repeatedly.

Suddenly, I felt my hands clasp the sides of my head, almost covering my ears. Was I trying to shut out the refrain? Was the refrain even coming from the outside? No, it was coming from inside me. *I* was shouting "my babies, my babies, my babies" to *myself.*

As I sat there, I felt my heart start to pound faster and louder. I felt an earthquake in my stomach. It was as though my organs were all spinning—one on top of the other. I started to sweat and my hands shook.

My body and mind betraying me, I felt a soft hand on my forearm. It was Shoua's. She didn't say anything, but she knew I was in agony. I could tell by the expression on her face.

Soon Melissa came over to me and started to talk. "Meetra, are you all right? What *mospoaeir notcjpaoer….*" Jumbled, incomprehensible words again.

My interpreter started to translate, but I don't remember what she said. A glass of water appeared, and I flushed it down. I was supposed to be observing a religious fast but I didn't care.

"ponitaon hieaps or poe ripoioo …" the sounds continued.

◆   ◆   ◆

I don't know what happened after that. I soon found myself on the bus, with Shoua sitting beside me. She lived on the northern side of town, but she was on *my* bus headed south. She was going to see me home. We didn't talk with one another. We couldn't, because we spoke different languages. Strangely, had we been able to communicate, I don't think we would have conversed much anyway.

As I sat there, looking out the window and watching streaks of buildings swish by, I was embarrassed by how my emotions had come unleashed. I thought about what I was going to do. I didn't know whether I was going to survive all this or whether I had lost the struggle and the end was imminent.

As timing would have it, just as I closed my eyes, Shoua placed her hand on mine. No words, just a touch.

I didn't open my eyes, but I also didn't pull away. I sat there still, more still than I had ever been in my life. I looked at nothing, I listened to nothing, and I felt nothing. I floated away.

In these still moments, the stillest of my existence, I heard answers. I felt icy resolve.

In these moments, my own truth spoke, and I made a decision to change the course of my life.

Iran
The 1960s and 1970s

My candle burns at both ends;
It will not last the night;
But ah, my foes, and oh, my friends,
It gives a lovely light!

Edna St. Vincent Millay

Chapter 9

The months and years on the calendar turned, and sooner than we expected my brother, sister, and I were young adults. We were growing more responsible for our choices, and the choices we made had consequences.

My first lesson in this reality was when Khosro came home one day from school and announced he was going to be a musician. Maman, who was hand washing a dark red shirt, said, without lifting her head, "No you will not." With that, Khosro became an orthopedic surgeon.

Finally able to channel their talents into productive endeavors, Khosro and Aram had become accomplished musicians over the years. Khosro was a master violin player. Aram played equally well on the santour, a trapezoid-shaped hammered dulcimer. The two had become famous in their school orchestra, both creating and producing a new school anthem. They even played regularly for broadcasts on Tehran Radio each week.

Maman took issue not with Khosro's talent, but with his future. Maman, like most Iranians back then, believed the only real way any man could be assured success in adulthood was by studying engineering or medicine. Other professions were a gamble, and my family was not the risk-taking type when it came to financial security. So Khosro had two choices, and he chose medicine. Just to get him to crack a smile, I told him he could tote his violin around the emergency ward if the business of doctoring got to him. Khosro just rolled his eyes, but I have to say the thought of him standing there in his white coat, balancing a violin under his chin, made me laugh.

Khosro learned to check his childish mischievous side. That said, he still wasn't shy. I'll never forget the summer he slept on our flat roof just about every night. While not entirely uncommon for people to do during the hot Persian summers, the night I decided to join him I realized the attraction. As I plunked down under the bright moonlight and warm breeze, I caught Khosro laying on his side, head propped on his hand, elbow bent. Motionless, he kept his head fixed west in Suehaila's direction. She was our neighbor who, at that moment, was climbing into her "harem-like" bed and untying her long, wavy black hair. As she tucked her dainty feet under the bedsheet and made sure the mosquito net was sealed around her, she plopped down about as gracefully as I had. From the look on Khosro's face, however, you would have though she lowered herself like one of our ancient goddesses.

Though Khosro's nights were full of distractions, his days were focused on academics. He had been admitted to Amir Kabir High School, which was renowned for its science program. He was on course to carry on the bone-setting tradition in our family.

One day, while we were keeping warm by the koursey, I threw a pistachio his way and asked him about the book that had been captivating him for hours. As the shell bounced off his page, he looked up and crinkled his face in amusement. After all, it had probably been ten years since he and I had been by the koursey, he spitting shells at me and I smudging tea-drenched raisins onto his copy book.

Remembering those days, he flashed a nostalgic smile my way. "What are you reading?" I asked him.

"It's a book on political ideology. I got it from Dr. Massoud." He cracked open the nut I had thrown at him and popped it into his mouth.

Khosro's teacher, Dr Massoud, looked just like an intellectual. He wore tailored suits like the ones Baba wore, but the patterns and colors were more muted. More academic. He carried a leather briefcase and smoked a pipe—a western pipe—not the kind Beebee enjoyed at Maman's expense. His hair was turning white and had started to thin. The kids used to laugh and attribute its recession to the countless times he rubbed the top of his forehead as he lectured us on philosophy. For hours at a time, back and forth his hand traveled across his head, the words spilling out of his caressed brain. Surely, we joked, this had to be hard on any follicle trying to sprout a delicate strand.

Like a lot of academics, he was also eccentric. What made him tolerable, maybe even appealing, however, was that on the continuum of eccentricity, he fell onto the half that was still dignified and distinguished. You could take him out and he wouldn't draw that much attention to himself.

Dr. Massoud's courses focused on Persian history and, more specifically, the accomplishments of the Pahlavi Dynasty now hosting its second king, Mohammad Reza Shah Pahlavi. What interested Khosro were the conversations the two had outside of class. Open political dialogue was discouraged—and, on a bad day, punished—so these conversations were private, maybe even clandestine. Usually, they started with Khosro taking a little longer than necessary to organize his notes, stack his books, and pack them neatly into his bag. While he took his time doing this, his classmates were filing out of the room, having packed up long before Dr. Massoud had ever finished lecturing. It was then, while lighting his pipe, that Dr. Massoud made his way through the aisles of desks, offering up some small talk and pleasant inquiries about how our family was doing. Once Dr. Massoud realized all this etiquette wasn't necessary, the two of them, along with any other students interested in talking off the record, started in on edgy topics like politics, the non-royal line, and religion. These conversations were generally moved off school grounds where overeager ears were harder to come by.

At this time in our nation's history, Iran's diversity of people was ruled by a monarchy. The population was divided by fortune, as well as by views regarding the traditional and western models of culture and development. The Pahlavis, who embraced Westernization and modernization, sought to make Iran into a regional and international power. This decision led to questions regarding the role of Islam, democracy, and civil liberties. These were the topics Dr. Massoud loved exploring when he was off duty. He wanted students like Khosro to contemplate a variety of contemporary political ideologies—most especially, the intricacies of communism. In fact, it was rumored that Dr. Massoud had not only rejected the Islamic practices of his family, but that he had actually, secretly, become a member of the Tudeh Party, Iran's communist party. Even more striking, there was talk that Dr. Massoud had not only known, but supported Mossadegh!

Mossadegh was elected prime minister of Iran in 1951, and while by most accounts he was a nationalist, over time the communist party came around to support many of his policies. In 1953 Mossadegh nationalized the oil industry, arguing that it was an Iranian asset and that it was unjustly controlled by western powers. His seizure of the oil fields created a groundswell of support among university students and faculty, evident by their emotional demonstrations in the streets of Tehran. Because some members of the Tudeh supported Mossadegh, there were also posters touting messages like "Long Live Lenin" and other pro-communist statements. In an even more dramatic effort to express themselves, some demonstrators marched towards the king's palace, wooden sticks in hand, chanting "Death to the Shah!"

While this confrontation did not result in mass revolution, the king and his family did leave Iran for fear of a leftist coup. Interestingly enough, while the nationalists under Mossadegh certainly had strong convictions concerning the role of foreign powers in the country, it was really the communists who had the strength, arms, and organization to pose a threat to the throne. Many even argued that the Tudeh were using the nationalists to launch their own takeover.

As the communist rhetoric intensified and gangs of supporters began looting the streets of Tehran, the West took notice. Iran was strategically important to the United States. To sit by and allow the Tudeh to heave the nation into the Soviet sphere of influence was dangerous. Moreover, it was an affront to U.S. foreign policy goals in the region. And so, with the goal of keeping Iran a U.S. ally, the CIA was sent to the country to overthrow Mossadegh and put the Shah back on the throne.

Once back at the helm, the Shah soon persecuted the communists and anyone else opposing the regime. Opponents of all kinds then went underground, priming themselves to counter the monarchy decades later.

The Mossadegh episode, coupled with additional readings about socialists like Mazdak, invigorated Khosro. Ultimately, though, his political discussions served to turn him into a capitalist instead of a communist.

Though enamored with Dr. Massoud and intrigued by communism, Khosro turned their conversations together into discussions about what lay ahead for Iran, the broader Middle East, and the world as a whole. More to the point, he and his teacher started to debate the issue of where the Third World would find itself against the backdrop of the growing East and West struggle.

As Khosro and I sat there by the koursey that day, Khosro told me about what he had learned. He believed Iran had long suffered from the self-serving footprints of Great Britain, Russia, and now the USSR and the United States. I remember how pragmatic his arguments sounded. He didn't think it was right that Iran had been subjected to the influences of so many countries over its history, but at the same time, he could see Iran for the resource-rich Third World nation it was. He knew the near future would not change the East–West competition barreling its way through the mountains and hills of Persia.

When all was said and done, Khosro believed the First World made the decisions, and the Third World took its orders. He decided he wanted to belong to the body politic of the First World.

"Meetra, *they* determine the outcomes. They issue the verdicts we wind up living with!" he told me as he shifted his weight and reached for a date. The brass bowl tipped as he pulled the fruit from it.

"Why?" I asked, cracking open a pistachio and sipping on my tea. A few tea leaves had sunk to the bottom of the glass.

"Because we are in the Third World, and they are in the First. Because we have oil, and they need it."

"Don't you think it might change? The Shah wants to bring Iran up. We were talking about this in class the other day." I said.

"Yeah, he does want to elevate Iran, but I just don't see how the United States and USSR are going to let him stray too far. They have their own vision of what Iran should be."

"Why are you so interested in all this? I thought you were going to be a doctor."

"Meetra, I hate to admit this, but I want to live where the decisions are made. I love Iran, our family, but I feel stifled here. Stuck."

"Where do you want to go?" I asked, surprised and a little nervous.

"The First World. West. Based on what I have read, I don't see communism having much of a future. It kills people's incentive to do anything. The West, now that is where the real freedom is. It is where you can make your own future—not the future your past gave you, but your own."

Khosro's voice emphasized and elongated the sound of "own." The word had a soul to it. When I heard him speak, I couldn't help but to look deep into my tea glass. There was a resolve in his words. An intention in his tone. Our family was on the verge of changing again. We were all making choices that were taking us up a flight of stairs neither Maman nor Baba had showed us the way to. We were climbing to rooms we had never lived in before.

Chapter 10

As the beautician yanked one line of hair from her face after another, I could see follicle after follicle plumping up in resistance. Irandokht didn't say a word, of course, but each time a fresh set of hairs were ripped from her raw face, she shuddered. I clinched my eyes shut. The beautician, on the other hand, never flinched. She continued on as though she were weeding her garden—she treated the hairs as though they were stubborn plants wrecking her backyard.

By the time we left, Irandokht's face looked like a baby's bottom does when it has a diaper rash. Sadly, she looked the same the next day, and though she tried to cover her wounded face with powder, the crimson color penetrated through.

Yes, as Khosro buried his brain in books and dreamed of the West, my sisters and I were marrying. The night before Irandokht's wedding, she went to the threader to have all the hair on her face plucked. All I can say is that night, I told Maman that she could just forget the whole *band-andaz* routine. My face would be fuzzy the day I married, and that was the end of the story. Before she could say a word, I said, "Oh yeah, and I don't care what people will say!" I then spun around on the edge of my heel and walked away. I heard Maman chuckle to herself. I was her daughter and she knew it.

◆　　　◆　　　◆

I may have been able to keep the hairs on my face from being snatched, but there was no avoiding the formalities of courting and matrimony. After Irandokht, I was next. Fourth in line and the last girl; Maman couldn't wait to loosen her girdle and close up the wedding shop.

Some guy who was related to Irandokht's husband became my husband. That's right, one day a man showed up with a fancy suit and change he jingled in his pocket when he felt nervous. Maman fluffed pillows and made lots of *polo* in preparation for his visit. By the time my turn had rolled around, everyone knew the drill. Maman was to sit and talk pleasantries with the man's parents, I was supposed to pop in and serve some tea, and my suitor was then to give me a once over and—if he was anything like Khosro—make sure my ankles weren't fat. I have to say that that day I deliberately wore a long skirt and boots that fit me to my kneecaps. Anyway, I was supposed to make an appearance, smile, and act coy. His parents would ask for my hand, and Maman, not wanting to appear too eager to unload me, would say she had to think about it. By this point, she had three experiences under her belt and moved through the exchange the way one plays a role in a choreographed play.

There was no reason to say no to my future husband, so my next memory was of the *tabagh-kesh* strutting their way down the street. Dressed in black pants, white shirts, and gloves, they carried heavy, rounded trays on their heads. All the gifts Maman had bought for our new home were on top, and as the tassels dangled in the breeze, the neighbors came out to gawk. I remember seeing the mirror, symbolizing trust, on the first tray, followed by trays of sweets, china, and silverware. Watching the men carry such large and heavy bundles on their heads gave me a headache. For Maman, watching all the items go by and knowing their cost made her head hurt.

So there I was with a husband deemed decent. I had made it through all the hoopla leading up to the wedding night. Obviously, I knew I was supposed to be a virgin that night—but no one told me there would be a *test*! Here I had a mother and three sisters, a brother who was going to be a physician, and no one had filled me in on this "minor" detail.

So, on my wedding night, as I lay there with Omar, he said, "Well, you've never ridden a horse or done gymnastics have you?"

Suddenly I thought of Tuyserkan—the last thing I thought I would be thinking about on my wedding night. A rural area, Tuyserkan had horses everywhere. They were the only real way to get around. Maman didn't know it at the time, but Khosro and I regularly snuck off and dashed about with one of our friends whose family owned many animals. Whenever I climbed onto a horse's bare back and dug my heels into its side, I felt free. I felt like it was only the two of us out there on the horizon, breaking away, escaping. I loved to wrap my fingers around his mane and feel the desert air comb the hair from my face as we sped along the open land. While I did know most girls never rode, I never thought this had anything to do with our prospects for keeping a husband! *Damn that Tuyserkan* was all I could think. The absurdity of our time there now took on new meaning.

"No, never been on a horse, and I can't even walk a straight line on the ground, let alone on a balance beam," I replied.

"Good. There shouldn't be any trouble then."

"Trouble?" I said, trying to sound blasé.

"Yes, my family can be really old-fashioned about that kind of stuff. They are pretty traditional. They rejected my older brother's wife because she had failed the virginity test. It was a shame actually. She was a good woman."

"*Rejected her*—you mean they sent her home, *back to her parents?*" I asked, sounding less blasé this time around. In that moment, I pictured being packed up and delivered back home to Maman. The thought was so scandalous my eyes stopped blinking and my limbs went rigid.

"Yes, very sad. She's still not married."

"Oh my God," I thought. Maman would go into an epileptic convulsion if she woke up one day with me on the other side of the door. Me, who had just failed my virginity test.

"Hmm," was all I said. What else could I say? Oh yes, there was this: "*Damn that Tuyserkan.*"

◆   ◆   ◆

Well, from there I carried out my marital responsibilities. Thankfully, the examiners were not in the room to investigate the state of my virginity. Omar was simply asked to display a bloody handkerchief as proof of my purity.

The problem? The stain was insufficiently visible to the audience below.

Chapter 11

Most people who have been married long enough can pinpoint moments when their spouse made a choice that either propelled the relationship forward or caused it to retreat. It is in these critical moments that an action, a choice, or a word can cause love to sprout or simply die away.

My first such moment with Omar occurred the night we married. While I had ridden horses in my early life, I had never done gymnastics. I did have a spirited side to me—even a mischievous one, perhaps—but I knew I had very little space to make mistakes. As a family without a Baba, a family with an already stressed out mother, and as a daughter who *loved* her mother, I never wanted to lapse in a way that would have irreversible consequences. In other words, except for the clandestine horse riding, I had followed the rules, and I *was* a virgin.

Why the handkerchief didn't oblige, I can't tell you.

In a stunning act of heroism, however, Omar did what I consider to this day to be the most chivalrous act of our marriage. As I lay there, imagining the scandal about to unfold, Omar got off the bed and made his way over to the chair in the corner of the room. I pulled the sheets to my chin as I watched him. Once by the chair, he reached into his coat pocket and pulled out a napkin that happened to be hiding a tomato from one of the *khoreshes,* stews, we had at the wedding dinner that night. He lifted the pieces and squeezed the juice from them. I watched the liquid stain the center of the handkerchief a deep red.

Wiping his hands dry, he then looked at me and smiled. I smiled back and we said nothing to one another. He then covered himself in an oversized robe, stepped out of the room, and flashed the cloth to our families below. I heard a clap and a sigh of relief. It was then I imagined Maman breaking out her fan and doing a belly-flop into the nearest couch. Finally, she would think to herself, her last daughter had passed *the* test.

When Omar came back into the room, I just stared at him. He smiled again, and I smiled back. We never spoke of this incident.

Kindness transcends language.

Chapter 12

Upon exchanging rings and kisses in front of our families, Omar and I did not know one another. In fact, we didn't even love one another, yet we had promised to stay together for the rest of our lives.

This reality, this rite of passage, was like a thin line of thread that served to tie me to my fellow countrywomen and ancestors of my past. Like them, my husband had been selected for me. While Khosro watched the 1950s musical *Picnic* and dreamed of freedom and falling in love, for me love was something that postdated marriage.

Maman taught me that ultimately love is not what binds a couple in the beginning or the end. Rather, shared values, personal compatibility, familial similarities, and supportive parents are the bookends that feed and sustain a successful marriage. Between these ends, then, is the love that grows out of time spent together and mutual commitment. Romantic love can't be the catalyst of a relationship, and it can't be expected to sustain it. If it comes at all, it only comes in time. I had no expectation that it should have shown up at the beginning of our relationship, and had it never shown up at all I didn't believe I would have been slighted. I had been taught that romance—at least the kind Khosro dreamed about as he watched Western movies—was overrated and fleeting, if present at all.

And so my marriage to Omar started with a basic compatibility, but no real love. I expected no more. Our wedding night and his effort to save my reputation, however, was the first of many experiences that would take me from indifference to something else. I had grown up in a world that saw only black and white. This was a world where "others" had decided who we were based on some criteria we had no part in setting. That night, had Omar left his tomato behind, I might once again have been labeled and dismissed. Omar stopped that from happening, and yet he worked within the constraints we found ourselves bound by. He had a grace about him, and when I saw this elegance for the first time, I exhaled like someone who has been running across the sand for miles and stops by the water's edge.

Throughout our marriage, Omar found ways to work both sides of a conflict. One night, for example, when we had invited company over, Omar wanted to serve some of our guests alcohol. At the same time, he didn't want to offend those who were strict Moslems and didn't drink. To solve the problem, he went out and bought tall, opaque glasses. That night, tea, Pepsi, and whisky drinkers all toasted to good health and no one was the wiser.

Omar was a bright man who had done well in school. He particularly excelled outside of the classroom, however, because once in the real world he was able to combine his book-smarts with his natural ability to bring people together. Omar absolutely loved to socialize and always left group situations more energized than depleted. Still, he was disciplined and rose each morning at five AM to prepare for his appointments and projects that day. He was a high-ranking official in the Shah's army, so this military post was a good match for his personality. It suited the side of him that was detail-oriented, regimented, and precise. The job also required that he work with groups that had a tendency to disagree more than collaborate. His affability built more roads than ravines.

Almost always waking up later than Omar, I would saunter down to the kitchen for my morning tea about eight in the morning. By then, Omar had gone through an entire pot and was well on his way to his next meal of the day. Sometimes he would look so tired sitting there hunched over his desk, papers in piles around him. As I would round the wall and ask him if I could get him anything, he would reach out his hand and draw me into his wide chest. Pulling my long hair away from neck, he would gently kiss me and ask me how I slept. Some days he would surprise me and ask me if I wanted to take a day trip out of the city. Omar had a hard time leaving his work behind, but on days he sensed that no matter how long he sat at his desk nothing productive was going to occur, he had the discipline to know it was time to let go and focus elsewhere.

Those days we broke loose took us to places all over the country. Sometimes we headed south where bright, open fields of white, yellow, pink, and red poppy flowers gave way to rows of date trees rimming the city of Shiraz. Once in town, roses lined the streets, and merchants tried to seduce us into their shops to browse. Colorfully woven carpets with distinct geometric shapes hung from everywhere in a city celebrated for its famous Persian rugs. At that time, the Shah was looking to make Shiraz the "Paris of Iran." Construction sites were set up every few blocks, and money was flowing in like an ocean current. Always an admirer of history, Omar couldn't leave the area without a visit to Persepolis, the ancient capital of the Persian Empire. As we walked along the perimeter and studied the ruins, Omar succeeded in convincing me to visit the Tomb of Hafez.

Once there, he would recite poem after poem he had learned in school. When I asked him how he had mastered the love poems so well, he said that he had studied up on them just for me.

Other trips included jaunts to *Menar Jonban*, the Shaking Minaret, and the Riviera Hotel in Ramsar. Located on the edge of the Caspian Sea, this hotel was lined with bright orange and lemon trees. What I remember most was the vast staircase connecting the beach below to a large patio. Here, guests ate under moonlight and spiraled and spun to the music until the sun came up. Guests were always dressed in clothes found only in the most exquisite boutiques of Milan and Paris. What's more, the women's ears, necks, and wrists flashed like stars as one husband after another whirled his wife around the floor and their jewelry caught the light.

In love with the shore as well, Maman too had taken us to the Caspian Sea as children. We, however, would stay in a neighboring town called Babolsar. Unlike Ramsar, home of the Riviera Hotel, Babolsar had no restaurants and was about two and a half miles from the sea. We were responsible for all the cooking and cleaning, but what I remember most of all was the fresh *nan*. Everyday we would head to the center of town where the smell of bread rose like plumes of smoke from the ovens. The baker had an oven right in front of him where he would bake the bread and sell it. I still remember him crouching down and slapping the dough against the sides of the hot oven. He used to plant his feet flat on the ground as he rested his chin on his knees. From there, he watched the dough turn brown and crisp.

The *nan*-maker was there year after year. Over time, deeper and deeper wrinkles lined his face until his young son, once only a dough maker, took his squatting spot and began slapping the *nan* against the hot oven. How jealous I was at the time that he didn't have to go to school like we did.

Chapter 13

"Zardee—man bar tou Sorkhie tou bar man ... Zardee—man bar tou Sorkhie tou bar man!"

"I leave the yellow color of my sadness and sorrows with you, and I shall carry your rosy and healthy vigor with me into the New Year."

As I put the lid on the rice pot and turned the temperature to simmer, I heard the chants. It was the last Wednesday of the year. Outside, people were leaping over the small fires they had set on the streets in celebration. In less than a week the calendar would flip to the first day of spring, which was also the Persian New Year, or Nowruz. A holiday that had been celebrated for over three thousand years, it was as grand as Christmas is in America.

Omar and I were having company that night, and I was excited. Whereas I had once dreaded Nowruz because our family could not afford the many gifts we were expected to give to others, as an adult woman blessed with relative wealth, it had become a holiday I adored.

For weeks I had searched through the fancy boutiques sprouting up in town, gathering bags of boxes stuffed with the latest fashions and home furnishings.

I had even found an elegant black dress to wear that evening for the party. It had a V-neck and a modest number of sequins that served to catch a subtle amount of light. I hated gaudy dresses and thought this was just the right balance between something elegant and something that looked like a glossy snake in the dewy grass. I also had a new pair of shoes—black and high heeled.

In anticipation of the party, the night before Omar had slipped a ruby and diamond necklace around my neck. Whereas the sequins I wore only caught a minimal amount of light, each time I took in a breath, the stones shone in brilliance. It was the kind of piece people noticed as soon as they looked at me.

In a last effort to straighten up, I took one last look at our *Haft-Seen*—the Seven S Table, as traditional as Christmas trees to Christians. It boasted all things starting with *S* relating to rebirth, renewal, and revival, the basic themes associated with Nowruz. The vinegar, signifying age and wisdom, had not yet evaporated, and the *sonbol*, hyacinth, welcomed spring by overpowering the vinegar's sour smell. As I glanced over the coins, lentil sprouts, and other traditional items, I felt a sense of pride.

Actually, this isn't honest. It is not honest at all. I didn't feel pride, gratitude, or any real sense of appreciation. The fact of the matter is that I felt conceit. I felt haughty. I knew that all my Nowruz treasures had been set on fine crystal and colorful, expensive china. I had paid a fortune for my spread, and I felt puffed up by its presence.

Ignoring the nag inside of me, I told myself simple pride was all I felt and allowed myself to be distracted by the doorbell. As I untied my apron and took it to the kitchen, Omar went to greet our first guests.

In a few minutes, our living room went from empty to swollen. People couldn't talk or eat fast enough. I stationed myself by the stove, filling dish after dish with mounds of steaming rice.

Many of our first guests were Omar's colleagues. I didn't know most of them all that well, but I had spent some time with several of their wives. The majority had come from families with money and talked readily about trips abroad and the fancy boarding schools their children were attending in Europe and America. Like mine, their clothes were haute couture, and their jewelry cost enough to pay for the food and education of ten of the orphaned children who lived a few miles away.

As they congregated in the kitchen and attempted to help, their conversations filled the air.

"Did you go to the Yazdis' party last week?" one asked.

"No, but I heard there weren't that many people there. They have a small house—not surprising."

"Well, we dropped by. She really can't cook. The rice was so sticky."

"Was Fatimeh there?"

"Yes, she had some rag of a thing on. She has really gotten fat—you should see her."

"Yeah, I heard. She had better watch it. Her husband will get some young thing if she's not careful," the woman said, sneaking a piece of *tadhig* into her mouth.

"What were her ankles like?" I felt like saying as I piled another layer of kabobs onto the tray. As the ladies continued, they tried to include me in the conversation.

"That's a lovely dress you are wearing, Meetra. Where did you buy it?"

"Oh, thank you. I got it at that new store downtown."

"Is that a new necklace too?"

"Yes, from Omar. He gave it to me last night." As I answered her and placed the last skewer onto the plate, I heard a roar of laughter coming from the men in the living room.

"Well, giving you jewelry like that could be a good or bad sign," one woman snickered.

With that, one of the other women in the room shot her a shameful gaze. It was more polite to talk behind someone's back than to her face.

I said nothing. As I picked up the tray and headed into the living room, I noticed it was even more crowded than when I had stepped into the kitchen.

The party went on for hours, and I got tired sooner than I had expected. Just before I headed back to the kitchen for some refreshments, I heard the doorbell. It was Farah. Taking a detour, I rushed over and kissed her on both cheeks.

"Salam! Eid-e-Nowruz Mobarak!" Hello, Happy New Year. It was not yet Nowruz, but I still greeted her with our national greeting.

As I helped her take off her coat, Omar came and said hello. While he made her feel at home, I darted to the kitchen and filled the empty glasses I had been carrying. As I looked out at Farah, I saw she was still standing. As she scanned the room and noticed the society women with their fancy pocketbooks, she seemed locked in place. She was dressed in a modest black skirt and a comfortable green sweater. Her shoes were flat. Among the painted faces, hers paled. She had powdered her cheeks and covered her lips with a shimmering light pink lipstick. Still, they stood out against the hot red color in abundance around the room.

As I watched her, a strange feeling came over me. Before I could identify it, a woman came into the kitchen and asked me for some sumac to sprinkle on the kabobs and rice. Temporarily distracted from Farah, I pulled the powder from the cupboard.

As I reentered the living room to find Farah, I spotted her across the way. She looked just like she had all my life. A friend of Maman's, she was a faithful neighbor and a devout Zoroastrian. I knew little about her religion, but I did know she always said that good thoughts, words, and deeds were the answer to life. When she prayed, those were what she asked God to help her cultivate.

Farah was sitting near the corner of the room where I had piled all the gifts I had bought for Nowruz. Against her plain skirt stood the red, yellow, green, and gold packaging. Bright rounded bows bent their way around the boxes' straight lines.

As I headed towards Farah, she stood and reached out for my hand. No sooner had she looked at me than her eyes fell on the necklace bursting off my chest.

Though her head only jerked a centimeter, her eyes said it all. She squinted ever so slightly, not because of the light beaming off the stones, but rather because of the years that had just flashed before her. I imagined her remembering me with flower bulbs in hand and a mouth that would not stop. I then saw her mind recalling the movies we had frequented and our talks about what mattered in life. *What was important.*

While I continued to talk to her through this bustle in my mind, I didn't even know what I was saying. All I could think about was how my life had changed. Changed in what seemed like a moment—the moment I married Omar and slithered my way into this layer of existence.

As soon as I could, I excused myself from our conversation and went to my bedroom. I stood in front of the mirror and looked at myself. Painted face and sparkling neck. I took a deep breath, looked into my own eyes, and then bowed my head. I used my long, colored nails to open the clasp of the necklace and release it from around me.

As I placed it in the velvet box on the dresser, I knew I would never wear it again. Then, I opened the drawer, moved the hair combs aside, and found my scissors. One after the other, I clipped off the tips of my nails. I felt a release. A renewed sense of autonomy washed over me.

That night, I learned shame can be a good thing.

Chapter 14

As I became less and less enamored with society life, Omar and I started talking about where our future, our story, was headed. Naturally, a discussion about children followed. These conversations started in the dark, where we were covered, protected, by blankets and the fairytale-talk of nightfall. As the months passed, however, the conversation moved into the light and showed up first at the breakfast table. Later the subject appeared at the dinner table, where our most serious disagreements always pulled up a chair and demanded notice.

It was when the talk of children clocked-in over supper that my stomach caught the kind of fire that fans the base of your throat. At first, I tried to smile and change the subject, but then, Omar's persistence also showed up. All I could do was bow my head, clutch my hands together, and pick at something invisible on my palm.

We were happy. We were safe and protected. Our life was secure. Why did we have to risk all that? Why did we have to disturb the rhythm?

Omar was different from me. I have never wanted to ask too much of life, to push it too far, because I know I will have to pay in the end. You only get so much happiness, so much security, before your quota ends and it's time to pay. This is how I saw things. How I saw life. Omar, on the other hand, thought satisfaction was overrated. He believed in pushing life and pulling out of it all you can. You push until it pushes back. You drive it to higher goals, loftier destinations. In Omar's world, good was good, but more was better.

And so, there we sat across from one another, trying to move that third chair away from the table. Deciding whether or not to have a baby offers no compromise position. If one spouse wants one and another doesn't, there is no middle ground. That said, I knew choosing not to have a child would be detrimental if not deadly to our marriage. This is to say nothing about how it would have been a cultural anathema. Our own king had divorced his barren wife over the issue of offspring. Children were the hope in our culture, the patch we clung to to get us from one place to another. Children make us want to survive—to build—Maman always said.

Some decisions in life are not really decisions but simply resigning ourselves to what we know we must do. Thus it felt when I "decided" to have a child. I told no one of my private terror, my fear that I was steering my life in a direction I couldn't control. I feared ending up with a life as difficult and desperate as Maman's. So while my friends delighted in buying little clothes for their own sons and daughters, I couldn't even get my nursery decorated. In fact, I couldn't bear to have the bassinet in plain view because it sent me into a panic. Months went by, and I never really thought about the life growing inside of me.

Time, however, has a way of slapping denial in the face. When little hands and feet poked at me from inside my belly, I began to worry. I worried about what would happen if I didn't love my child as a mother should. I feared people would know I was faking motherhood. I terrified myself with questions about what kind of adult my child would turn into with a mother like me!

Fairytale nights turned haunted.

◆   ◆   ◆

"I am so sorry," I said to Omar, reaching across my body and resting my hand on my sore abdomen. I had just woken up from labor. The doctors had also done surgery on me and removed my uterus when they could not stop my body from bleeding.

"Sorry for what?" he asked.

"I know this means I can't have any more children. *You* can't have any more *with me.*" I said this in a tone of voice that signaled he could have an "out" if he wanted one. As though I knew this turn of fate was a bad one that did not bode well for our family. I said it this way because I wanted clues. I wanted to see if he saw this event as one that would change our marriage, our commitment to one another. I didn't have the courage to ask him outright, but my inflection and the look on my face suggested I knew this could be the end of what we had known together.

"Meetra," he began. "We have a son, and you are all right. What more can a man ask for?"

"But you love children. I know you wanted a houseful."

"Life doesn't always respect our plans. Childbirth is dangerous business in our part of the world, Meetra. There are never any guarantees. I am just grateful you are safe, and our son is well. The whole time you were in labor I worried I might become a widower—a widower because I pushed you to have a child you were reluctant to even have. Life has provided well for me. I am grateful, and I am blessed. I love you."

With that, he leaned over, touched my cheek, and kissed me. We never spoke of this issue again.

◆   ◆   ◆

If ever there was a miracle in my life, this was it. The day before Behrooz was born I resented motherhood. The day after, I became a mother. As I wrapped my arms around his wiry, jerky body, I realized I couldn't get Behrooz close enough. As he started to fuss, I took my thumb and rubbed the spot between his eyebrows. He immediately quieted and relaxed in comfort. That was the exact moment I became who I am today. It was the day I started soldiering for my child.

Behrooz grew faster than I ever wanted. The bittersweet blessing in having an only child is that every first is a last. Because I knew I would not have another baby, I was hawkish about savoring every moment. I wanted to log and stockpile every memory, as I knew any given scene would never come around again.

The intensity of this reality often proved overwhelming. I hadn't been prepared for the ferocity of emotion that came with Behrooz's arrival. As each day passed, I felt sad I would never get it back. This sentimentality went on for months, and I coped by cuddling and carrying him everywhere we went. Whenever he fussed, I tried to find that spot between his brows like I had when he was only hours old.

In time, life has a way of bringing things into balance. Toddlerhood was the counterweight that pulled me back from one puddled set of eyes after another. Behrooz started walking at ten months. From there, *he was off!* He loved his new legs and was not up for cuddling with his mom much anymore. He rarely sat down, preferring to just squat when he needed a rest. In general, he enjoyed his own company, playing with his toys and our plants for entertainment.

When he turned about fifteen months old, he found a new pastime—throwing tantrums. I still remember how he heaved himself onto the floor and pressed his head into the carpet, outraged at the injustice of not getting his way. Sometimes my blood pressure soared with each carpet convulsion. Other times, I was quietly entertained, like when I saw him peek up from the carpet to see if I was watching him. When he was finished I would say "*boose, boose*, kiss, kiss," and he would come over, mouth wide open, and bury his face in mine. It took months for him to learn to kiss with a puckered mouth.

I also remember cooking away in the kitchen, only to feel little arms wrapping around my legs and a ball of a head barreling into my thighs. Then there were the nightly baths. When I turned on the spigot, Behrooz would lift up his hand and try and catch the stripe of water sliding out of the pipe. He didn't understand why he could see the line of water and yet not capture it. After a few tries, he would look up at me for an answer. I would just smile, and he would smile back, trusting in the mystery of it all.

Of course, we had rough days when his teeth drilled their way through his tender gums and he howled in pain. Other days, he paused in his newfound mobility to come into my arms. These days were few, so when he laid his head on my shoulder and folded his arms around my neck, I stopped what I was doing and drank in the moment.

As those early months and first few years passed, I found myself deeply in love with my new son. Too, I was curious about the man he would become. Would he have a personality like me, Omar, Maman, or even Baba? What would he care about in his life? What gifts had he been given? I was excited by the possibilities, but I also knew that because he would grow up and away faster than I ever wanted I needed to trust life to provide answers in its own time.

◆   ◆   ◆

So, the 1970s were good to our family. We were happy, healthy, and in Omar's case, professionally successful. His skills and talents had taken him so far that he wound up closer to the Shah than most others. We were living a blessed life.

During this time, Khosro was called to the West. He was able to secure an orthopedic residency abroad, and we all knew he had to take it. With a toast to Beebee Jon on his last night in Tehran, Khosro packed his violin, the few hundred dollars he had saved, and Maman. Persian moms go with their eldest son, and so Maman, who had never expected to relocate, got a passport.

Khosro told us that one day he might return to Iran. We knew better. Those who went West never came back. As we started to say good-bye to one another at the airport, he stashed some pistachio shells in my coat pocket.

"Make sure Behrooz learns how to pitch these correctly. It's all in the tongue."

My eyes filled. Once Khosro turned his back to us, when I knew he would only be looking forward, I leaned in to find Omar's soft touch. He put his arms around me and stroked my cheek. In my peripheral vision I could see Maman tottering her way along on her bowed legs. She had her arm looped through Khosro's and was headed towards the gate.

Behrooz, not really understanding what was going on, stood beside us and waved good-bye to the two. He looked confused by the farewell. Nevertheless, he just kept waving his little arm into the empty air. He would look in Khosro's direction, and then pivot his head to me, hoping I would explain it all. He was searching for clues, something to give context to the scene. All the while, his little fingers kept motioning forward, scrolling the air in farewell.

Just watching my sweet baby say good-bye, *for forever*, brought fresh flip-flops to my stomach. Behrooz gradually came to sense something sad was going on. With that, his enthusiastic hand went limp. He stopped waving and made a dash for my thigh. I felt this head burrow its way into me, and I reached down for his soft curls.

Iran
Late 1970s

There is in every true woman's heart, a spark of heavenly fire, which lies dormant in the broad daylight of prosperity, but which kindles up and beams and blazes in the dark hour of adversity.

Washington Irving

Chapter 15

It was the late 1970s, and the bad years were back. We just didn't know it yet. Although the decade had opened with good health and fortune—Behrooz was growing up and enjoying school, and Omar's reputation and position in the military was secure—much was in store for us. My life had been going along well too. I had pulled away from a lot of my society "friends" shortly after Behrooz's birth and proceeded to fill my time with family, books, letter writing, and gardening.

Irandokht lived close by, but sadly she had been unable to have children. She and her husband had visited countless doctors, but nothing ever came of it. With the shut of the last exam room door, Irandokht decided that if this was God's will for her, she should dedicate herself with the full force of her spirit to the less fortunate children in our community. She connected with various nonprofit and religious organizations in town and wound up spending her days in the trenches of the city helping to bring proper meals, literacy, and shelter to the thousands living in poverty. Like the milkman of our youth who worked into the dark hours of each day, she too committed herself to the vulnerable as though her life, not theirs, depended upon it. After a long week, she would often come by on Friday afternoons and flop into our couch.

"How did your week go?" I asked Irandokht, handing her a mug of tea. It was nice to entertain family; I could skip the formalities of fine china.

"Up and down. We got a new child on Monday. Her mother died in labor with her brother, and her father was killed in an automobile accident months ago. She is two. Her eyes are as wide as the mouth of this mug. She was stiff when I first picked her up. She couldn't settle in. By the end of the week, I couldn't get her out of my arms. Every time I rested her on her own feet, she burst into tears and pulled at my dress." Irandokht sipped her tea thoughtfully. "I need to find some clothes for her. She only has one set. Do you think one of your *friends* might have some stocked away?" She pronounced the word "friends" in a sarcastic tone.

"I don't know. I'm sure someone does—I'll ask around," I replied.

Behrooz came into the room. He had his favorite puzzle in hand. When I saw him grinning broadly, I thought of how Omar always said he looked like a big smile on legs. Once Behrooz spotted me, he darted over and plopped his head on my lap. A clap of wood sounded as the puzzle pieces fell to the ground and bounced off one another.

Glancing up, I was not surprised by the expression on Irandokht's face. She looked at Behrooz with a foreign eye. Unlike the children who had clutched her skirt all week, he was clean, cared for, and loved.

"He is a lucky child. Blessed," Irandokht noted.

"Yes." It was then I paused and considered bringing up a subject that had haunted me for a long time. It was a question that, after I became a mother, was not just philosophical but deeply personal.

"Do you ever wonder why …?" I started. I paused with reservation.

"Why what?"

"Why it's like this? Why are some children, by virtue of birth, set up to make it, while others, due to the circumstances into which they are born, are not?" I took a sip of tea and helped Behrooz straighten a puzzle piece into place. Sensing that Irandokht wasn't ready to respond yet, I continued. "I mean, why is it that the children you work with are suffering so much? They are just as deserving of love and support as Behrooz. All children come into this world the same. One just as deserving as the other. Just as innocent. If that's the case, then why is Behrooz here, playing with a puzzle, and that little girl you just told me about is downtown, a hungry orphan? Moreover, why are some countries unable to find the peace needed to allow their citizens room and opportunity to grow? Children born in some places in Africa are doomed just because they came into the world there! It isn't fair! Every child is as deserving as another. Why do only some get a chance? Doesn't this drive you *crazy?*"

As I spoke, my voice turned taut. I struggled to breathe in enough air to feed the words barreling out of my mouth. Although Behrooz couldn't understand what I was taking about, he sensed my frustration and crinkled his face in concern. My monologue of protest made him whine and slap my face with his tiny hand. He knew I was upset, and he wanted me to stop talking, to end my outrage. I had turned raw, and he didn't like it. I took his tiny hand in mine, kissed his palm, and told him everything was all right. He quieted.

"I don't know, Meetra. You have always had so many questions. You think so hard about things. Sometimes there are no answers," Irandokht said.

I knew she had a sentence or two left in her, but I interrupted anyway. "Irandokht, I am asking *you* how you process all this. How do you make sense of it?

Because, for the life of me, I can't! Every time I see a needy child I see Behrooz's face. I am infuriated by the inequities! Life can turn on a dime. You and I certainly know that better than anyone. *Why*—why should innocent children suffer?" By now, my voice had elevated again and Behrooz grabbed my mouth. Without intending to, he sank his thin, sharp nails into my skin.

"I don't have any answers." Irandokht started. "All I can say is that—"

My emotion got the best of me again, and I interrupted her. "Where do you see God in all this? Where is he? What is he doing *experimenting* with us?"

"I don't think it is an experiment, Meetra. And God *is* with us. He is with me every day I dredge up the energy to go to work and carry one more child on my worn and tired hip. He is with me each day that I find the patience to settle one more traumatized toddler. He is with me at night when I find the strength to let it all go until the next day, when I'll wake up and start all over again. God is with me at each step. That I know." She paused to think. "As for answers to all the bigger questions, I don't have them. I don't think I ever will in this lifetime. Sometimes, that is the best we can expect—the knowledge that some answers will be left to another time and place."

"How do you live with that kind of ambiguity?" I asked.

"I don't have a choice. Besides, questioning will not help me help the innocent. Those kids need my full attention. *Khoda Bozorg-ast*, God is all powerful. I know this. The rest is out of my hands."

With that, we each took a sip of our tea. There was nothing left to say.

It was a good thing that God had guided Irandokht instead of me into looking after our nation's most vulnerable.

◆   ◆   ◆

In that way, life went along, and while most of us were engrossed in the issues that directly affected us, a storm was brewing in the political world.

For some time, various groups across Iran had been registering their complaints about the Shah's regime. Diverse criticisms sprang from pro-communist, pro-democracy, and pro-Islamic groups alike. There were others, I am sure, but I remember these groups most clearly.

Since coming to the United States, I have gone back to read about this period in my nation's history. Before I tell you *my* story, however, I'll tell you the story of my country. After all, although I didn't know it at the time, our stories would intertwine and be forever fused. We shared in the good times together, my government and me; as the late 1970s approached, we would be traumatized together as well.

◆   ◆   ◆

The Iranian Revolution of 1979 actually has its roots in prior decades. I lived most of my life under the monarchy of Mohammad Reza Shah Pahlavi. His government was technically defined as a limited monarchy because we were permitted to vote for members of the *Majlis*, or parliament. He was a secular king, however, whom we all referred to as the "Shah."

The Shah had inherited the throne from his father during World War II. Like his father, he dreamed of growing Iran into a formidable regional—and, if possible, international—power. He had received some of his education in the West, so he was not only familiar with western values but believed some of these principles and practices could help modernize Iran and build its prestige.

In the 1960s, the Shah had launched the White Revolution, an economic and social reform movement. The government invested large sums of money in development projects, land reform, redistribution initiatives, educational endeavors, literacy campaigns, and suffrage. Women were granted the right to vote and other legal concessions. The judiciary was transformed. Traditional clergy were often replaced with more secular judges who, under orders from the Shah, refused to outlaw controversial vices such as gambling, alcohol, and premarital sex. In short, many clergy lost their long-held influence and power. When they rose up in revolt, the Shah imprisoned them in places from which they would never again emerge. To help stifle public discourse about this, the Shah also banned all publications considered slanderous and blasphemous to the regime.

Over time, as the Shah's modernization efforts gained momentum, some of the traditional clerical groups in the country grew resentful. First, a large number had lost land in the redistribution drive. Many more were unhappy with the infiltration of western values and customs. These included everything from the new fashions many women sported to the nonindigenous music and entertainment that flowed into Iran. Debates about the proper position of women in a traditional Islamic society took place, as did overarching discussion regarding the role of Islam in the nation's culture and political institutions. Secularizing the nation's laws and customs offended the religious and long-entrenched classes in Iran. Some clergy equated modernizing the country with westernization and thus rejected both. Of course, not everyone believed this, but the traditionalist message resonated in significant pockets of the nation.

In addition to religious opposition to the Shah, some liberal secular groups wanted to see a weakening or abolishment of the monarchy. These groups accepted some westernization but criticized the Shah for not allowing western *political values* to infiltrate the country. They demanded more open dialogue, a less censored press, free speech, and the guaranteed right of citizens to criticize their government. These opponents of the Shah were often university students and intellectuals, the middle and upper classes, and the urban elite.

Whereas the clergy resented the government for its endorsement of western *values*, the democratic reformers demonized the king for his close relationships with foreign powers and for the subsequent influence these nations had been allowed to wield in Iran. The secular critics started by criticizing Great Britain and Russia for their meddling in the early part of the twentieth century. Next they turned on the United States for its interference in the 1950s Mossadegh affair. Ever since, they believed, the United States had both used the Shah as a puppet and created SAVAK, an intelligence organization intent on brutality.

SAVAK (*Sazeman-e Ettelaat va Amniyat-e Keshvar*, or Organization for Intelligence and National Security) had been trained by the CIA. SAVAK was charged with protecting the Shah and his regime. There were numerous accounts of vicious, even deadly, measures SAVAK officials took to squelch opposition and protect the king. The secret police were basically given full rein to arrest, detain, torture, and surveil citizens in the name of national security. Such techniques led the Shah's secular, western, educated, and urban opponents to condemn the regime they lived under. They were equally angry with the West, but despised its foreign policy escapades in the region rather than its beliefs and principles.

What the democracy activists shared most with the clergy was outrage over unfair allocation of the nation's wealth. Many Iranians believed that the Shah and his people were squandering Iran's money and personally wallowing in its comforts. The 2500-year anniversary of the Persian Empire had been an infamous symbol of ostentatious decadence. The anniversary, held in Shiraz in 1971, was a three-day party that cost over three-hundred million dollars. Over one ton of caviar was served, and many elite chefs were flown in from Paris for the affair. It had been a massive undertaking for a Third World country, and the Shah was roundly criticized for spending money in this fashion when there were hungry and homeless citizens in need across the nation.

So, liberal secular groups joined with clergy to oppose the Shah. In addition, some Marxists, working alongside Shia clergy, sought inspiration in the revolutions of Algeria and Cuba. They too wanted a different Iran. In short, a lot of angry people felt they had no viable political outlet for their frustrations.

Then came the year 1978. That autumn, the policies and practices of the past culminated in a series of demonstrations against the Shah. I don't remember all the events, but on September 8th—also known as "Black Friday"—a large number of people protesting in Tehran were met by the full force of the Shah's military. Some of the soldiers defected to the protesters' side, but enough stayed on and used their helicopters, tanks, and machine guns against their countrymen.

In December, two million people met in Azadi Square to protest the regime. Still more military officials and soldiers switched sides, but not enough to bring the regime down. At this point, the Shah did try to loosen his hold on the country, and some reforms occurred. These changes came too late, however, and the nation spiraled downward. The many protests and demonstrations were causing serious economic disruption in the country, as wages were frozen and the funding for many projects terminated. With significant numbers of Iranians losing their jobs, many who had not yet opposed the Shah turned on him.

On January 16, 1979, the Shah and his family were forced from the country. Many leaders had been executed in the past, and he of course feared he would be next.

On February 1, Ayatollah Khomeini returned to Iran after years of exile and proceeded to establish the Islamic Republic of Iran. Khomeini became head of state and claimed a lifetime tenure. He was also known as the "Supreme Spiritual Leader" of the nation.

Despite general agreement that the Shah had to go, the many opposition groups did not agree on what kind of government should follow the revolution. In short, when the religious clerics won this battle, the country went from a secular nation to an Islamic theocracy.

One year later, Iraq invaded our country. Thus began in an eight-year war with our neighbor. When all was said and done, conventional, chemical, and biological weapons maimed, deformed, and killed over a million of us. Missiles rained on our cities, and death was everywhere.

This was the country I found myself in. This is where I lived.

Chapter 16

So, what did all this mean for my family and me?

This:

Omar was killed.
Irandokht was killed.
Behrooz was in danger.
I almost lost my mind.

Omar, Behrooz, and I were driving out of the city.
An enormous truck crossed the center line.
Omar swerved, but we crashed.
I opened my eyes.
My dead husband's body was sprawled across me.
My baby had been ejected from the car.
He lay limp on the street.
A flash, a loud crunch, our life as one ended.

Irandokht and her husband were arrested.
They were detained.
I visited them in prison, and we exchanged cryptic notes.
They told me they would soon be free and wanted to go to Shemiran to rest.
I imagined them escaping.
I imagined a reunion.
The next day they were executed by a firing squad.
I buried their bodies in Shemiran.

Everywhere I went I was followed by *pasdarans*, the Revolutionary Guards.
I was a threat to the regime.
Behrooz turned nine years old.
He was barred from attending school.

He fell behind in his studies.

The Iran-Iraq War raged.
We mothers exchanged stories.
News.
Information.
Children as young as ten were being drafted.
They served as human waves.
Sometimes, the children would be tied together in a line, twenty children to a group.
Tied so a lone child could not run in fear.
Across the minefields they walked.
Mines blew.
Children blew.
The tanks then crossed.
There was a war to win.

Chapter 17

It was now officially winter. The empty tree branches poked the crisp blue sky, and flakes of snow powdered the sidewalk. In the past, I had always welcomed the change of season and had especially liked winter. I loved lighting a fire, crawling under a thick blanket, cup of tea and book in hand. All my life books had served as an escape and a voyage. I could be transported to any place and time within minutes of hearing the spine of a novel crackle. Excited, I knew I was going somewhere the real world could never take me.

That day, I was positioned in place, ready for the afternoon's trip, when all I could do was lie there. My tea tasted like warm brown water, and the book felt like a bundle of nondescript papers. Behrooz was in his bedroom where he hid himself regularly. He was playing—at least that is what he would always tell me. Often, when the game seemed like a long one, I would tiptoe upstairs, rest my ear on his closed door, and hear him whimpering. As I opened the door, I would see him in a fetal position on his bed, fists tight and tucked under his little chin. Whenever he saw me come in, he would smear his tears from his face, shoot up, and pretend he was fine. Funny how even at the age of nine he felt pressure to take life's pain "like a man."

That day, I walked over to the bed, sat down, and just held him. His fall from manhood to boyhood was rapid and startling. With my arms around his shaking body, he howled out for his father.

At that moment, with my baby clinging to me, I made the biggest decision of my life. The stillness in me finally broke, and a declaration came forward. A dictate.

When I heard the words, when the path opened up, I felt a sense of resolve and relief. Since summer, Behrooz and I had been padding around our home in a fog. We had been disintegrating before one another. I decided that no matter the outcome the stupor we found ourselves in would end. One way or another, it would all end.

Chapter 18

Making the decision to leave your country is like riding a seesaw for the first time. Terrified while rising into the air, you feel momentarily safe when your legs touch the ground and the hard wood slaps the dirt. Then, as you are swooped back up into the air, you realize you could grow accustomed to life elsewhere as well.

On the one hand, I could see that Behrooz and I were spiraling into a dark and impaired existence. We barely spoke to one another, and we rarely left our home. I tried to lose myself in my books, but every time I got a paragraph or two into my novel, my mind would drift, or I would grow incredibly sleepy. I could not sleep well at night, yet I could doze off easily on the couch with my book.

Behrooz grew almost silent as the months passed. Normally, the presence of people energized him and he became gregarious like his father. He had always been responsive to others and enjoyed talking with just about anyone he could trap into a conversation. He was also sensitive, and when others hurt, he felt it too. Though I failed to see it at the time, I know my pain sank deep into his bones. A close neighbor of ours had even told me that Behrooz had approached him about getting a job. He told him that with his baba now gone, he had to take care of his maman. The neighbor kindly let the boy sweep his front step and then later told me of the exchange.

This conversation with my neighbor occurred the morning I decided to leave Iran. The day I decided we were going to escape.

◆　　　◆　　　◆

Choosing to leave was no simple decision. Conversations I had with friends flooded my thoughts. *Everyone* was talking about what the revolution meant and what they were going to do.

"Maybe the *mullahs*, clergymen, can turn things around. Bring things into balance for a little while," said person "A."

"Yes, the other day, I heard someone say that even if they just offered a counterweight for a while that would be beneficial," person B said.

"I don't know," C said. "I think we are headed for trouble."

"I agree," D said, taking a puff of his cigar. "There is all this talk of equal rights and democracy, but I am not sure the mullahs are going to let it all play out that way. I am really thinking we need to consider a counterrevolution if things turn sour."

A piped up again, raising his hand in protest. "Ah, no counterrevolution. The mullahs are right—we have become too western, and the Shah was in the pocket of the United States. Jimmy Carter was running Iran. Our own culture and national interests have gotten lost. I think we'll be able to work with the Ayatollahs to move forward and reclaim some of our history and national pride.

"I don't think so. I think we are headed into dangerous waters," E said.

"What do you mean?"

E continued, "I just keep thinking about civil liberties, the rights of religious minorities, women … the list goes on and on."

B started in, "Well one thing is for sure. We have to stay vigilant. Engaged. Those families that are escaping, they are *cowards*! *Absolute cowards!* Who do they think they are, just up and running out? Abandoning their country. It is offensive and immoral!"

"Yes," A said. "And, morals aside, it is totally counterproductive. If everyone who cares about what is going on, especially those who oppose the revolution, were to leave, who would be left? Only those who support the revolution and those too vulnerable to do anything about it! How will the country ever have a chance of changing if those who *can* change it refuse to help? If those who *can* change it flee in fear?"

"Absolutely, B, I agree with you. We can't leave. This should not be an option."

With that, everyone around the table nodded their heads and grunted, "Yes, *Afareen!* Bravo!" That was about the only thing we could agree on as the conversation continued long into the night.

Even though many of these conversations occurred in my living room, I listened more than I participated. This last thought regarding what would happen if we all left stayed with me the longest. Growing up, I had believed life to be black and white. I believed in certain ideals, and I believed that only a person lacking integrity turned away from his ideals. I believed we each had to stand for something, and that the faint of heart who did not would be forgotten by history. The key to life had seemed clear back then. The answers came easily, and I had no tolerance for those who made the choices appear murky.

But now, with my shattered life as a backdrop, there I sat, faced with having to reconcile my two selves: one that believed in standing up and the one contemplating escape. My mind swelled with questions. How would I honor the lives of those I had lost by leaving? How would that make my country better? Did running *ever* solve anything? Better yet, what right would I have to criticize my country as a non-citizen? An exile? Moreover, how *dare* I come back to Iran if I had not worked to create the nation I returned to?

What if all the grand figures in history had run? Isn't history made by those who were fearful but carried forward in spite of their fear? Dying for a cause, for a belief, was *celebrated* in our children's textbooks. Irandokht didn't run. She looked a firing squad square in the face and stood there as bullets exploded in and around her. By virtue of having worked for an outlawed religious group, she was declared an infidel. She could have abandoned her work, left the orphans, but she didn't. She was steadfast and honorable to the end.

But then, Irandokht was gone. My precious Omar too. Where had their ideas and loyalty gotten them? It got them dead. It got them to the gravesite I dug for each one of them. Was their resolve noble or just stupid? Had they just given in, gone along, and made concessions, would they be alive today? Had they just sat down, *shut up*, and ducked their heads, would we be the united family we once were? Was it all worth it in the end?

My God, the questions came faster than any of the answers. Words circled my brain, my fists tightened, and my body throbbed with anger. What were we supposed to do as humans on this earth? What beliefs should we enslave ourselves to? What was paramount? Ideas? Survival? Protecting our children? *What?*

I felt like a hypocrite for contemplating escape. I knew I would be betraying my younger self by running. I was an embarrassment and an insult to myself, because when the stakes were high, I lured myself into walking away.

Indictments swarmed my mind for weeks. I hated my life and the choices that lay before me. I felt paralyzed by the daunting task of deciding what to do. I also feared that in doing nothing I would be making choices as well.

Just when I thought I would never find the answers, I found myself at the kitchen sink one day washing the breakfast dishes. It was a mostly cloudy day, but out the window I saw a few sunny places in the yard. While rubbing the dish sponge against a crusted plate, I suddenly heard a child scream.

Quickly, I looked out the window and saw a little girl who could not have been more than two years old flat on the pavement. Just minutes before I had been watching her and her mother stroll down the street, stopping every so often to pick up a leaf or small creature walking the same path. The little girl would take a few steps before confidently quickening her pace to a skip or a run. Her mother warned her to be careful, but as I well know, children that age love their freedom. Apparently, her little legs had gotten ahead of her and she had fallen flat on the ground.

Her cry and the sight of her mother rushing to her side stopped me cold. Behrooz was older now and no longer cried out like a toddler, but I was still sensitive to the sobs of a little one. As the mother peeled her child off the pavement, frantically searching her face for scrapes and sores, I was taken back years in time. At that moment I knew one thing for certain.

I was a *mother.*

Chapter 19

So in the end, it was the mother in me who prevailed. She won.

I would devote the next months to planning our escape. I would get Behrooz out of the country, even if it killed us both.

◆   ◆   ◆

My days of planning were driven by fear of my new country. I was terrified that my son would be drafted into the war. We were not welcome in our country any longer, and as if this were not enough, my baby was in jeopardy of being asked to clear landmines with his child's body.

Iran has always been a country where news and information travel best by word-of-mouth. Traditionally, this is how we have survived and made important decisions. Since information on escaping is not something you advertise, this informal network proved invaluable in helping me make the connections I needed.

Someone whom I knew knew someone else who knew a Baluchi guy. Baluchis come from Baluchistan, a territory in southeast Iran shared with Pakistan and Afghanistan. Through my informal network, I learned that Baluchis were smuggling Iranians into Pakistan. The price they charged was exorbitant—but then again, that was the price of freedom. I asked the Baluchi man to visit our home. I asked him to help us escape.

◆   ◆   ◆

It was about ten at night, and Behrooz was asleep. It was the only way I knew how to protect him from the conversations and decisions of that night.

There was a rap on the door, and I opened it. Before me stood Mohammad, the man who held all the cards. He was tall, heavyset, and had a long and wooly beard. He didn't smile but just mumbled something as he entered the house.

As is customary, I brought a tray of tea and cakes out for us to share. Mohammad barely glanced at the fresh sweets before him, but he stared for a long time at our rugs and other furnishings. I had hidden some of our belongings, but you can't hide everything.

His mind was full of numbers. Dollar signs. A blaze of anger flashed through me.

I waited for Mohammad to initiate the conversation. When he did, although I had a difficult time understanding his accent, I knew what he was saying.

Basically, he could get Behrooz and me out, but it would cost us everything. If I wanted to be smuggled into Pakistan, I needed to provide him with copies of all my financial accounts, withdraw all our money, turn over my household items to him, and pack a single bag for the two of us. We would have to follow directions explicitly. Obedience was cardinal. Any "funny business" and we were "done." Translation: dead.

I had the strangest feelings towards Mohammad. He was our lifeline, which endeared me to him. He was also a stranger who ran a business and who saw me as a good investment. He was in it for the money, and I only had his attention because I had some. He was not loyal to me—he was loyal to his business.

Ultimately, my feelings didn't matter. He was our chance out of this place. And so, I motored forward.

◆　　　◆　　　◆

Several days passed before I saw Mohammad again. Just when I thought I might need to find another smuggler, he came knocking on the door. Barely over the threshold, he demanded to see my bank accounts. There was no socializing.

I brought the account information to him, and he handed me a new passport and travel documents. He took my Iranian passport and then waved his two buddies into the house. With a twirl of his finger, he instructed them to roll up the Persian rug in our living room and carry it out the door. Not only was it an expensive rug, it had sentimental value as well. Omar and I had purchased it during one of our trips to Shiraz early in our marriage. That rug going out the door represented the "good years."

As I watched the burly men pack up my memories and walk out the door, I felt a fresh ooze of adrenaline—the bad kind. This was only the beginning of the process. *Our lives* were walking out the door, and there was no turning back.

I stopped myself before I could feel too much. I had to shut off my emotions until I saw us to Pakistan. Only one thing ultimately mattered, and that was focusing on getting my child and me out of Iran.

Mohammad followed the two men out the door and told me to pack one suitcase that I could carry. He would be back at three AM the next night to pick us up. Oh yes—I was to give him all the cash I had and leave the house as it was. If any of our belongings were missing, the deal was off.

I suddenly imagined my special things in a Baluchi hut, or up for sale at a bazaar, next to a hanging chicken.

Chapter 20

One bag. I was to walk out of this country with one bag and my son.

You might think it would be hard to decide what to take, but it was not. I packed as though Behrooz and I were going away for a week, because that is all you can fit into one suitcase.

I thought about going through my house once more, opening every drawer cabinet to hear it creak shut one last time. I knew my house so well that when I heard a door close, I knew exactly which one it was. Each had a different tone. Same with my kitchen drawers and bathroom cabinets. I knew which stairsteps creaked and which windows opened easily to the outside. Every book and knick-knack on my shelves had a history. I knew what was in my pantry and what items I was running low on. I had even made a mental note to get some more milk and sugar when I went to the market. Funny, it didn't matter now.

Some of the best years of my life had passed by in this house. It was where Omar and I had created a family. It was where we had *become* a family. Here was where Irandokht had come to relax after a long and exhausting day of taking care of our nation's children. Here, Behrooz was born. Here was where he felt safe.

I stopped there. I refused to think about all my memories with Behrooz. I knew I would crumble in pain. I packed our suitcase and waited for Behrooz to wake up the next morning.

Our last day in Tehran was much like any other day. I decided not to take that one last farewell look through the house. Rather, I abided by my afternoon ritual of book reading and napping on the couch. I had made some bread for the journey, but making bread was a familiar weekly chore. Behrooz played in the garden and knew nothing of our upcoming escape that night. He was too young to understand it all. Before he went to bed, I told him to sleep in his clothes. I then told him that several hours later, a man would come to take us on a trip. I told him we were going on vacation for a while, and that he needed to listen to everything I said.

I also made him swear not to talk with anyone. Our plan was to pretend that he was mute so that we would not have to worry he would say something that could endanger us. You would think that asking your child to pretend he was impaired would invite his questions, but strangely enough, Behrooz asked nothing. He was a child, but he knew we were living in a dangerous world. He knew he had to trust me.

I kissed him goodnight on that spot between his eyebrows, and as I walked out of his bedroom and pulled the door shut, I heard a creak. A fresh ooze of adrenaline surged through my body. I felt nauseated.

◆   ◆   ◆

At three in the morning I was standing at the back door waiting for Mohammad. He arrived on time and came inside. I handed him my cash and he thumbed through the bills, making sure it was all there. He asked where Behrooz was, and I told him he was sleeping and that I would bring him down.

As I climbed the stairs, a reflex in me sounded. "It was a bad idea to leave a stranger in my living room unattended," I thought. "He could steal something right from under me." The second this territorial instinct in me was aroused, I realized that it didn't matter if Mohammad was alone downstairs. All my belongings were now his anyway.

I rubbed Behrooz's face and woke him. "Time to go," I whispered. He rose and descended the stairs. As he put on his shoes, I felt a rush of emotion. Who would have thought an old shoe-rack would be *the* possession that meant the most in the end.

Iranians do not typically wear shoes in the house, so all of our family's footwear was stored on a low bench beside the back door. When we came home we laid our shoes there, and when we exited we picked them back up. For years this little bench had guarded our shoes well. Once Behrooz had learned to scoot around on his own as a baby, he had been fascinated with this little shelf. It was a perfect height for him, as the upper shelf was only twelve inches off the ground.

Behrooz was forever visiting the bench. He thought the top shelf, which registered about waist level for him then, was a perfect table top for his many toys. Time and again I had tried to get him away from the area, as the shoes were dirty and the floor hard and worn. I even set up a fence, but whenever I forgot to replace it, there Behrooz would be playing. When he was about one-and-a-half years old, he started finding his own shoes in the mix and bringing them to me. This meant he wanted to go outside.

The most sentimental memory I have of our shoe-rack occurred when Behrooz was ten months old. Having crawled his way over and hoisted himself into a standing position, he proceeded to knock all the shoes off the rack. I could hear them tumbling as I worked in the kitchen. Like Maman, wooden spoon in hand, I headed around the corner to reprimand him. As I looked down, he had his own tiny shoe in his little fingers and was smiling broadly. He offered it to me, his one foot stepping forward—and then the other. For an instant, he remained standing, beckoning to me put the shoe on his foot.

It was then I leaned forward, wrapped my arms around him, and lifted him into the air. *"Your first step,"* I cried. *"You just took your first step!"*

◆   ◆   ◆

Such memories seemingly arise from nowhere. That was the one that stalked me on my way out the back door. With Behrooz's hand in mine, I pulled the heavy wooden door shut for the last time in my life.

Chapter 21

Our next move was to board a small plane bound for Chabahar, a city in the southeast section of Iran on the Gulf of Oman. Still holding hands, Behrooz and I took our seats. The short ride was uneventful. This was the easy part.

Our first smuggler, Mohammad, had left us at the airport, telling us that a man named Abdul would meet our flight and see us into Pakistan. I was not told the entire plan; pieces of it were revealed to me as I made each step. Not knowing the big picture made the trip frightening, but on the other hand I could only worry about one stretch at a time.

When we got off the plane, Abdul was waiting for us. He took us to a hotel for the remainder of the day and told us he would be back at nightfall to pick us up. The rest of the escape would be over land.

That night Behrooz and I laid on top of blankets on the bed, not sure whether the sheets were any cleaner. As the hours ticked by on the clock, I fingered my hands through Behrooz's short, coarse hair. His breathing patterns suggested that he too alternated between sleep and wakefulness. With my heart pounding in fear, I told him we would be fine. "Soon," I said, "you'll be playing in the hot Pakistani sun." I don't know if he believed me, but as his mother, I had to reassure him even if my words were based more in hope than in fact.

At six o'clock the next evening, Behrooz and I waited outside the hotel for Abdul. Minutes later, he appeared from around the corner in a beat-up, dented, dusty jeep. That vehicle had a story of its own, this I know. Behrooz and I climbed in. Just before Behrooz sat himself down, Abdul instructed him to get into the back and hide himself under a wool blanket. We didn't ask why—we just followed orders.

We started driving out of the city and kept going for what seemed like hours into the night. As the scenery turned rural, I assumed we were now deep in the back country of Baluchi territory. As dawn approached, I could see animals and various hut-like houses plunked down across the landscape.

After hours of bumping along the horizon, we pulled into an area that had been settled by a Baluchi tribe. As soon as Abdul turned off the engine, children and wives came out to greet us. Behrooz waited until we cued him to appear, but when he did, he was just as mute as I had instructed him to be. I prayed he could keep up his silence.

The plan was to stay with the tribe several days while all the necessary arrangements were made. Meanwhile, I could take a crash course in Baluchi culture and customs. After all, I was to become a Baluchi wife. I would be posing as Abdul's wife during the escape.

"Here, this should fit you," an old Baluchi woman said, appearing out of nowhere. In her outstretched hands were the clothes I would wear for the remainder of my time in Iran. She handed me some loose trousers and a shirt-like hand-embroidered top. I took the garments from her and bowed my head in thanks.

She then leaned in and said something about my hair. I didn't understand her until she pointed to her own head as an example.

"Ah, a middle part," I said. The woman smiled—a breakthrough. She handed me a comb, and I arranged my hair like all the other Baluchi women I saw.

Around the village, lots of people were just sort of hanging around. There didn't appear to be any industry close by. Now I understood why the smuggling business was the hot game in town. Soon, the same old woman tapped me on the shoulder from behind. As I turned around and said hello, I noticed a young girl with her.

"I am her granddaughter," she said, pointing to the woman. "I can speak Farsi."

"Great, so glad to meet you," I exclaimed. The old lady said something in Baluchi, and the girl translated. "Would you like to have some lunch with us?"

"Yes, thank you." I followed the women for a few yards to a large tablecloth that had been laid across the ground. As I sat down on a thin pillow, a puff of dust blew out from under my billowing pants. In front of us, dishes of rice, lentils, and barbecued lamb sat atop the plates. I knew Baluchi cuisine shared some similarities with Iranian fare, but as I looked at the color of the oil lining the edges of the plates, I guessed turmeric and paprika had also been married with chili powder and hot red pepper. When Behrooz coughed just after swallowing a mouthful of beans, my suspicions were confirmed.

"Tea?"

"Please. Thank you."

"My other granddaughter, her sister, is getting ready to marry soon," the old woman said.

"Wonderful. Congratulations."

"Yes, she will enter seclusion soon. I will have to think about what I want to tell her."

"I'm sorry?" I said, trying to understand what the woman was saying.

As the girl translated, I bit into a piece of bread and watched a goat walk by. We stared at one another, both thinking the other was out of place.

"It is our custom," the girl continued. "Before a woman marries, she is placed in relative seclusion. She can only be visited by her close female relatives and friends. We are supposed to help prepare her for marriage by teaching her what she needs to know to be a successful wife and mother."

"What a wonderful custom!" I exclaimed, suddenly forgetting about the goat, who had now moved towards me, both eyes on my bread.

"Yes, this is a common practice among some of us."

"I think that is a great custom!" As the words left my mouth, I was taken back in time to my wedding night. My culture had no such custom. It was unlikely that any Baluchi woman here would be finding out about the virginity test on her big day! I chuckled to myself, and the goat looked up at me. I then chuckled at him.

Just as I turned my head to the old woman filling my plate with rice, another young woman appeared from behind. In her arms she held a tiny newborn baby.

"Ah," I exclaimed, melting with memories of Behrooz as an infant. "How old is he?" I asked.

"Four days."

"What is his name?"

"No name."

"Sorry?" I asked confused.

"*Sasigan.* On the sixth day." Bewildered, I looked at my young interpreter.

"We name babies on the sixth day of life," she said.

"Oh, I see." As I bent my head to drink my tea, I thought of some of the anthropology books I had read. All the world over, customs like this existed. I always wondered if they were coping mechanisms—ways of dealing with high infant mortality rates in developing areas. Cultures—*mothers,* that is—had to be insulated from this pain. After all, it is crippling to think your little one could be snatched up before she ever even had a chance.

Not knowing what to say, I looked up to find the goat. Just when I needed him, the bugger had taken off.

While I was learning about Baluchi history and culture, Behrooz had begun playing with the slew of children he found company with. I had not seen him play like that in months and welcomed the sight. At first, I was nervous about releasing him from my watchful gaze. After a few days, however, I felt relatively secure and let him run about. All the while, I never heard a word out of him.

Instead, he had started to develop an interesting set of hand signs to communicate with the other kids. They were all learning from one another. Although I missed Tehran, there was something revitalizing about being out of the city, away from the TV and the politics of our time.

After four days with the Baluchis, Abdul told us the following night we would leave for Pakistan. Fresh adrenaline shot through me, and I nodded my head. I was to pose as his wife, and our story was that we were headed to Pakistan to see relatives. Like Behrooz, I was not to speak, lest anyone discover that I spoke Persian and not Baluchi.

That night, I sank to the floor for a few hours of rest. As I laid there using my *chador* as a blanket, I clutched Behrooz's hand and closed my eyes. I don't think I ever fell asleep that night. I tried to channel all my energy into being strong, courageous, and steadfast. *Nothing* but getting out of the country mattered at that point. I promised myself I would do what it took to see us to the other side of that border.

Chapter 22

Before I knew it, before I was ready, it was time to go. Dressed in the Baluchi trousers and oversized top I had been wearing for days, I draped over myself a chador, now required by law in Iran. While I may have been posing as a Baluchi woman, Islamic law dictated that regardless of culture or religion, all Persian women must cover. Sweating already, I pulled the large, black, robe-like garment over me and walked out of the hut with Behrooz.

Again, Behrooz was to lie in the back of the jeep while I sat up front with my "husband." It would be impossible to try and hide Behrooz, and so the plan was to pretend he was a paraplegic so he would not be seen as a candidate for the Iran-Iraq War. Poor child: I had declared him mute, and Abdul had cast him as disabled.

As I climbed into the jeep, I prayed like I had never prayed before. I didn't feel like I knew God, but I begged him for mercy, for life, and for a breath of freedom.

Ever since the revolution, I had been fighting to understand the waves of change that had swept over my life. Like a swimmer struggling against the ocean current, I too had been working against a tide that was drowning me. I had eventually channeled all my energy into planning our escape until, when I finally shut the back door of my house for the last time, I stopped slaying the waves and simply started to float. I imagined myself lying on my back in the Caspian Sea, face skyward. When I concentrated hard, I could feel my arms and legs go limp as I let the waters carry me wherever I was meant to arrive.

It is strange to look back upon that aimless, floating feeling. At one of my life's most crucial junctures, I loosened my grip and acquiesced. But then, if you have ever found yourself in the middle of a trauma, you know the feeling. In such times, you either come hysterically undone or you go flat. You float. There is nothing in between until the crisis passes. Only then does life make room for you to feel a normal range of emotion.

On we went into the night, driving across the desert without headlights so no one would see us. We swerved for reasons I still don't know, and we stopped every so often so Abdul could pay his respects to the local chief. Behrooz and I stayed in the car during Abdul's visits. There, under the dark, starlit sky, my mind jumped like a bug from one memory to another.

I thought about a Sufi dance performance Omar and I had seen one carefree night in Tehran. The dancers wore pointed hats and billowing green cloaks that were cinched at their waists. They began the performance in a circle, reciting ancient Persian poetry. Then they rose, spread apart from one another, and began moving in a circular motion. Their movements were synchronized in perfect harmony with one another as they arched their backs, tipped their heads, raised their right hands into the air, and placed their left hands on their back. They whirled faster and faster and entered a trancelike state as the music played on. Perhaps this was their version of my "Caspian Float."

When I got thirsty during the jeep ride, I thought of my childhood and Khosro. After Baba's death, he had been responsible for making sure the family had clean water each week. Along with Maman, he woke at three in the morning to head outside and greet the water the city had sent our way. Bleary-eyed, he and Maman followed the stream as it rolled down the *joob*, a narrow channel dug into the street for exactly this purpose. Eventually the water reached our below-ground *aubanbar*, our water chamber, where Maman sat making sure the tank didn't overflow. Once filled, Maman then dumped salt into the container to keep it clean. Khosro always wanted to know why they had to get up so early when the water was still running at daybreak. That water, Maman would tell him, you would never want to drink.

When I thought I saw Abdul coming out of the hut he had entered hours before, I felt my heart flutter. I then felt shame. For some reason I didn't understand, I was attracted to him. He had complete power over my life. I was drawn to him because of this power, and yet I felt disgusted by the very thought of him. My thoughts turned to Omar. Although he was a stranger to me when we married, Maman had been right about him. Time, experiences, and commitment had brought us to love one another. Without our realizing it, threads between us had been woven. We had created a family together and thought our lives indivisible from one another. Nevertheless, we were separated on that night the truck had barreled its way through us. Officially an accident, I knew better than to believe the collision was not intended to happen. Omar had been loyal. He had always been loyal to me and anyone else he had pledged himself to. That loyalty had been the death of him.

Sitting there thinking about my childhood, the twirling dancers, and Omar, I did finally see Abdul actually come out of the hut. I watched him swagger toward the jeep and fiddle with the door handle several times before successfully opening the vehicle. *Taryak*: opium. For the rest of the night, his foot jumped so abruptly between the gas and brake pedals that I got carsick and threw up.

Driving by night, hiding in local villages by day, and starving ourselves for fear of contaminated food and water, Behrooz and I made our way to the border. How long it took, I can't tell you. My days and nights were all mixed up, and I could swear some of Abdul's opium had clouded my mind by osmosis. Some-how, however, by the grace of God, I looked out the windshield one day and the border was in sight. The time had come. This was it.

There, with the line drawn in front of me, Abdul proposed marriage.

Yes, he wanted another wife—and he picked me. *Me.* We could barely com-municate, but perhaps that was the charm in it all. Most American men say they can barely handle one wife, let alone two or three. Perhaps Abdul was catching on to the complications of married life too but had decided that adding another one to the mix would take the pressure off tending to his spouses at home. There I sat, a wedding proposal hanging in the air.

All I could think was: my life is *literally* in your hands. Behrooz's life is in your hands. There is the border. *I can see it.*

To insult Abdul would not have been a good idea. To marry Abdul would have been an even worse idea.

Buy time—that is all I could think to do.

So, out came the story of how I did want a husband. After all, what is a single woman to do in this life? I nearly choked when I said this. I told him that I did need to see Behrooz into a boarding school—unless, of course, Abdul wanted to help me raise my son?

With twelve children already, the thought of a thirteenth put a damper on the romantic flare of the moment. With a break in the momentum, I told Abdul that once Behrooz was in school, I would search him out, and we could visit and marry in Pakistan. He liked that idea, because then all his wives would not be in one place. Not even in one country.

We drove on in silence for a few minutes.

◆   ◆   ◆

By the time we could almost see the border guards, we had endured several mechanical breakdowns, a fuel leak, and an estranged romantic relationship. With only minutes left to the checkpoint, Abdul stopped the car and turned off the engine. He placed his hand deep into his pocket and pulled out a large knife. He then uncovered Behrooz and poked the point of the blade into his neck. He pulled the knife back to show me its razor-sharp edge. He then put the blade back to Behrooz's neck and grabbed him by the hair.

"I want more money! You must give me more money," he whispered in rage. He was so close to me I could see the tiny capillaries in his eyes. His breath stunk of garlic.

"I don't have any—I gave you everything I have. All the money in my accounts and all the furnishings in my house. I have *nothing* left." I said in a controlled panic.

"No, you are *pool-dar,* wealthy. You have more, and you are hiding it. I will kill your son." He poked the knifepoint harder into Behrooz's neck. Behrooz jerked his head back in horror.

"Please—please! I have nothing to give you. Have mercy—please have mercy!"

"Give me your wedding band—*give it to me*!" he whispered.

I ripped the ring off my finger as though it had no meaning. Actually, at that point the only meaning it had was our salvation. I implored the ring to save Behrooz and me from this madman.

Abdul took the band, looked at it, and then buried it in his shoe. He said nothing. *After all that, he said nothing.* Behrooz burrowed himself under the blanket again. We were within walking distance of the border now. I tightened the chador around myself and took one last look at Behrooz. We locked eyes and said much. We exchanged no words.

Chapter 23

Abdul turned the jeep back on and took a very deep breath. Once more, he instructed me not to say a word. He would do all the talking for us.

One car was ahead of us when we reached the checkpoint. As we waited, I felt my heart pound. I wanted desperately to turn around and look at Behrooz, but I knew this would look suspicious. Sweat started pouring out of me. In a counter-intuitive move, I pulled the chador closer to me, as though I were cold.

The guard waved us up. Slowly, we drove toward him. I bowed my head, making eye contact with no one.

Abdul handed the guard our paperwork. Another guard came up to the jeep and propped his foot on top of the tire. He looked at Behrooz and asked what was wrong with him.

"Paralyzed and mute, *bee chareh,* poor thing," Abdul replied, tsk-tsking and shaking his head.

"What happened to him?" the guard pressed on.

"He was born this way. God never willed him to walk. His mother takes good care of him though, she always has."

"Where are you going?" the first guard asked us.

"Karachi. We have relatives there."

"What relatives? What's the address?" the guard asked in a pointed and accusatory manner.

"My brother and his family. Their address is ..."

I didn't catch the address and suspected it was fake, of course.

"Is that your wife?" the questions continued.

"Yes, sir." I never lifted my head.

"When are you coming back?"

"*Inshallah,* God willing, next week," Abdul replied. The second guard circled the jeep two or three times and peered into the vehicle more times than I could count. Just as the first guard was about to wave us through the checkpoint, the second stalled him.

"What is it? He seems fine to me," the first guard said. He had lowered his voice but I could still hear him.

"I don't know—I can't put my finger on it," the second guard said in a suspicious voice.

"Come on, it's getting late and I'm hungry. Let them go."

"I don't know—something isn't right."

"I'm tired and hungry. Let the tribesman go."

"*Okay, okay!*" The second guard said, rubbing the back of his neck with his right hand.

The first guard motioned us to pass through the checkpoint. Abdul moved the car forward and passed over the border. As he started to accelerate, I heard a shout.

An indictment.

A charge.

"He's a smuggler. I know I've seen him before. Stop him. *Stop him!*"

From there, all I heard were bullets. Bullets hitting the jeep. Bullets hitting the hubcaps and tires. Abdul slammed the accelerator against the cold, hard floor, and the jeep choked, laboring to comply with his demands.

Abdul had one hand on the wheel and one wrapped around his head. My instinct was to jump into the back seat and lay my body over Behrooz. Instead, I yelled for him to get onto the floor. To duck and cover his head.

With each second the car managed to gain speed. With each meter's distance from the border, the bullets subsided, and the lights from the checkpoint dimmed.

When I was finally able to turn around and see Behrooz, I saw that in fact, he had been able to make his way to the floor.

Yes, he was on the floor—and he was bloody. He lay on the floor, his eyes closed. Not closed as in scared. Closed as in not with us.

I screamed as though it were all over. As though it didn't matter that we had reached Pakistan. As though this moment would forever hold me in bondage, despite the fact that I was now free.

Greensburg, Michigan
The 1980s

The grand essentials of happiness are:
something to do,
something to love,
and something to hope for.

Allan K. Chalmers

Chapter 24

As I shuffled around to gather my things and get off the bus, I turned to Shoua and said "thank you" in my best English accent. I wanted to convey my deep appreciation to her, and I wanted her to know that her kindness that day—the day I broke down in Sewing Circle—had meant something. Something significant.

After I thanked her, she smiled broadly, patted my hand and said, "you okay?"

"Yes" and a smile were all I could offer back. Once off the bus and on the sidewalk, I waved. Still smiling, she waved back, nodded her head, and blinked in a way that said, "Go forward. I know, but go forward anyway."

When the bus had turned the corner, I walked toward my apartment building and pulled open the screen door that was still only half attached to the frame. I walked up the carpet-stained stairs, put my key into the lock, and entered my apartment.

I made my way to the kitchen and filled the teakettle. I broke my poverty-inspired rule about having chai only with company. I sat down at the table, pulled a napkin out of my purse, and unwrapped a cookie I had half eaten at Second Chances.

Outside, the leaves were changing. I couldn't decide which ones I liked the best. The yellows were warm, reminding me of fresh sunshine and long summer days. The reds were rich, conjuring up thoughts of fire and cooler days to come. They twirled around and around before the ground broke their fall. Whether we lived in a "good" or "bad" neighborhood, the city gifted us with large trees that had been planted decades before. Throughout Greensburg, we walked around, necks bent, faces to the treetops in awe. Yellow, orange, green, and red. Puffs of color slid, blanketing the streets and sidewalks.

As I sat there looking out the window, my eyes traveled to a large bush up against the side wall. It was the color of a brick on fire. In fact, I believe it was called a burning bush. Its vibrance and beauty startled me, and as I studied it, I started to cry. I cried like I had not cried in years.

I thought of Omar and how desperately I missed him—how I missed his touch. Starting out as separate strands in life, we had become knotted together. I shivered as I struggled to remember the lines on his face, the sound of his voice, and the curves of his hands. As I thought about what had happened to him, to us, I heard the sound of crunching metal all over again—I felt his hot blood pour out of his body and sink into mine. My stomach raged with the memory of leaving him there in the cold, callous ground. Leaving him under a gravesite I could never visit.

My face soaked with tears, I thought of Irandokht—her goodness, her purity. Why? was all I could ask. Khosro had said that it was best not to report her execution to Maman, who was too fragile to take the loss of one of her own babies.

Then there were my two older sisters who had stayed on in Iran. Their children were raised, and they had made peace with the new country. When I had told them I was planning on escaping, we had said our good-byes. Though we hadn't admitted it outright, we knew we would never see each other again.

Khosro, who was in Europe, worked tirelessly to get Behrooz and me a visa. The bureaucracy was relentless and the process extremely expensive. I know he was crazed by what had happened to our family. In the end, despite his best efforts, I was granted admission to the United States before Europe, and so I came here.

How strange. We all started out in the same house, the same womb. Maman's womb. Now, revolution and war had flung us into the land of the living or the dead. We now lived on separate continents. In our early years, we had been like spokes connected at the center of a wheel: separate in our identities, but tightly joined and close together. As time passed and revolutions came and went, we had moved apart, radiating out just like the spokes. Now we were at the farthest ends of the spokes where they reach the rim of the wheel. How had all this happened? How could we be so distant from one another when we had started out so close?

As I blotted my face and shifted in the chair, my eye caught a word on a piece of paper in front of me. The paper had been sitting there for days, but that word, its power, had escaped me.

"Refugee." I was in America because I was a refugee.

◆   ◆   ◆

"Refugee," a term used widely in the English language, actually has a specific legal definition, and it is used to describe all the people I have told you about so far. Miriam, Shoua, Aneesa, Nhu, and the others at the Sewing Circle were all refugees.

According to the definition in the 1951 United Nations Convention Relating to the Status of Refugees, a refugee is someone who, "owing to a well-founded fear of being persecuted for reasons of race, religion, nationality, membership of a particular social group, or political opinion, is outside the country of his nationality, and is unable to or, owing to such fear, is unwilling to avail himself of the protection of that country ..." In other words, a refugee is in jeopardy of *dying* because of what she believes, what religion she subscribes to, or what ethnicity she was born into. In contrast, had she been born in this country and held the same beliefs or been of that ethnicity, she would be protected by the U.S. Constitution. Because she is in a country without civil liberties, however, she is in danger and thus a refugee.

Eighty percent of the world's refugees are women and children.

We were refugees. I was a refugee.

And so, although I had an entire life in Iran preceding the revolution, my husband's job—along with Irandokht's charity work with a minority, and ultimately outlawed religion—put my own life at risk. This is to say nothing of the reality that Behrooz could have been snatched into the army at any moment. I had to escape. And so, hand in hand with a crooked Baluchi, through the desert I traveled until I reached Pakistan. Once there, like other refugees, I made my way to an agency that could help me gain the legal status I needed.

As a refugee, I had three basic options available to me. I could return to Iran if and when things settled down. I could stay in Pakistan if the authorities allowed me to. Or, I could be resettled by a third country.

Assisting me was the United Nations High Commissioner for Refugees (UNHCR), which has offices all over the world. The UNHCR works with governments like that of the United States to identify and resettle a small fraction of the world's refugees. When all is said and done, less than one percent of us are ever resettled by a third country. An even smaller fraction of this one percent is permitted to enter the United States.

Thankfully, at the time, I didn't know the statistical likelihood of *not* being resettled outside the Middle East. Nevertheless, when I was given an appointment to interview, I showed up a half hour early armed to argue my case. I was a refugee, and now I needed to convince "them" I was one.

I was asked questions about my life, my experiences, and my political affiliations. With the twitch of a hairy man's mustache and a signature, I was put on the list with others seeking resettlement. In a matter-of-fact way, I was told my next home could be in Australia, the United States, or a country in Europe. Busy shuffling papers, my interviewer told me that I could basically be resettled in any part of the world and in any city in a particular country. Such decisions were up to the agency and the government that had agreed to take me. He then signaled the next woman to come forward. I shook his hand, nodded my head in gratitude and walked out of the building. This was the beginning of three hard years in Pakistan. The beginning of the wait.

◆   ◆   ◆

When I think of Pakistan, slideshows of unrelated memories fill my head. I think of a blazing sun burning my skin as I shopped in the open market. I think of the smell of sweet curry, garlic, and milky tea, or the sound of merchants bustling about trying to lure customers to their stands. I think about how hot my tiny apartment got when I boiled rice for dinner, and I think about my neighbor's children and how they cried every night when their mother pulled the door shut and left for her second job. Her husband had married another woman, a younger woman. For the time being at least, she was able to maintain custody of her son and daughter. That would likely change in a few years. They would be stripped from her and given to her husband for good.

More than anything, I think of the hospital. Doctors in a little room sheltered my son for the many months following our escape. Behrooz had been shot by the border guards. Upon entry into Pakistan, Abdul drove us straight to the hospital and dropped us at the door. I gathered Behrooz in my arms, and as his blood soaked a larger and larger circle into my blouse, I thanked Abdul. The look on his face told me I would never see him again. Strangely, I felt relief and fright at that very thought.

From there, the memories blur. A gurney appeared, white coats were everywhere, and a lovely round-faced woman with a ruby in her nose enveloped me in a hug and escorted me away. Behrooz would stay in that hospital for six months, and I would use just about every last cent Omar and I had saved over our lifetime to pay for his care. The remainder, little that it was, paid for our living expenses. Yes, the smugglers had taken the bulk of our fortune, but I was Maman's daughter and a businesswoman in my own right. Before ever contacting Abdul I had sold some of my jewelry sent the money to Pakistan so it would be there waiting for us.

Although I may have had some of Maman's street smarts, on the days I laid next to Behrooz nursing his wounds I wished I had more of her strength. In the prime of my adult life, I was now a widow; more painful than that, I was in jeopardy of losing the one person who meant more to me than anyone else in the world. Some days I cursed my choice to escape, which had brought us to this hospital bed. Other days I knew had I stayed in Iran, the ruby-nosed nurse would have just been substituted for one in a chador who spoke Farsi. In other words, Behrooz's life would have been in danger either side of the border.

As the weeks ticked by, I found myself thinking hard about Maman and the trepidation she must have felt trying to insure that we all met adulthood with good health, wisdom, and the knowledge that she loved us. Behrooz was a boy now, but as I thought about these things I found that familiar spot between his eyebrows and stroked it the way I had the first day I had met him. I'd like to think this was the secret treatment no doctor could prescribe, the healing he needed that brought him back to me.

◆　　◆　　◆

When Behrooz was finally able to leave the hospital, we would occasionally venture out to shop or admire the buses. Behrooz was enamored with the bejeweled caravans that navigated the busy streets. Each one was more decorated than the one before, with neon and gold-colored paint and palatial ornamentation. As Behrooz got stronger and bolder, sometimes he would ask a driver if he could see the inside of one of these buses or trucks. They usually said yes, and as he ascended the stairs his eyes would widen. Some interiors resembled parlors, with billowing curtains, throw pillows, photographs, and decorative mirrors. Such buses were a sight I had never seen, and although I came to prefer the simple, functional European coach, I loved to watch Behrooz scan the streets for these vehicles. Every time he spotted one belching and swaggering its way down the street he would yank my sleeve, squeal, and point with zeal.

◆　　◆　　◆

More than three years after my first interview at the UNHCR office I was called back for an appointment. A woman with a tight bun pinned to the base of her neck told me in a very matter-of-fact manner that there was a spot for us in Greensburg, Michigan. Our plane ticket would be paid for by a revolving fund, she said, but once I started work in the United States I would be required to repay my travel expenses.

With a smile-squished face and teary eyes, I said yes. "Yes, send me to America."

That is how, out of the millions left behind, we became the fraction of one percent given a chance to start over. With the approval of the U.S. Congress and the president, I entered New York in the early 1980s as a legal immigrant. By the time I had stepped off the plane, I had been subjected to background checks, medical exams, and other inquiries designed to ensure I was deserving of refugee status. Moreover, I was evaluated in terms of my ability to work, support myself, and contribute to American society.

From there, we were connected to Second Chances, one of many voluntary agencies across the country resettling refugees. Once cleared in New York, we were put on a plane to Greensburg. I was instructed to display an emblem-clad blue-and-white plastic bag when I disembarked from the plane so that my case worker could identify me. Doing exactly as I was told, I placed that bag in front of my body like a shield when I entered the airport lobby. Not knowing English, I could communicate with no one, and so this bag spoke for me. As during my escape, I was completely at the mercy of those telling me what to do. I had to trust that the people I had met and the process I was engaged in would deliver me where they promised. I had to believe that I would turn up where they said I would.

The bag did its job. Within a minute of stepping out into the waiting area, a young, smiling woman came over and shook my hand. We made our way to the luggage carousel and picked up the one suitcase I had brought to the United States. Behrooz and I then followed her to her car, got in, and traveled across town to the apartment the agency had rented for me.

It was about eight PM when we arrived. Only one outside light was lit. A young girl whirled around the parking lot on a beat-up bike, and the balconies clinging to the side of the apartment complex held old, musty couches and broken appliances. Worn clothes draped the railings. In one unit, a man in an undershirt stood in the doorway clutching a beer. When he saw me he just stared.

My caseworker helped me with my suitcase as we made our way to the second floor of the complex. The hallway was scantly lit and smelled like mildew, its gold and white wallpaper peeling. My apartment number was 2B. The caseworker put her key into the lock and opened the door. There were two rooms. A card table and two plastic lawn chairs were set near the stove. Two other chairs sat in the living area and a mattress lay on the floor in the bedroom. When the caseworker opened the refrigerator, I saw eggs, milk, some bread, and a few other things I couldn't make out. She told me she would be back the next day to take me to an orientation. Then she said good-bye and closed the door behind her.

The following day I was taken to Second Chances and, in the span of about two hours, told about life in the United States. I can't remember much of what was said, but I do remember that I was required to get a job and pay my way within a matter of months. With limited English under my belt, three weeks later I was taken to interview at a hotel and hired that day. Each morning I was expected to report to work at six-thirty AM, which meant getting up at four to be ready to catch the first of two buses I needed to ride to get across town.

◆　　◆　　◆

Sitting there on the lawn chair watching the leaves fall, I had now been in the country six months—the point at which I was expected to be fully independent and functional. As the plastic legs of the chair bent under my shifting weight, I looked around at my dingy apartment and then back at the cherry-colored bush outside. It was then I felt a surge. A hot gush sprung from my heart and radiated out through my limbs.

I felt rage turn into resolve. I felt horror and despondency transform into determination. I witnessed my outlook shift from the dull colors of my apartment to the scarlet color of that bush.

Looking out the window, one more burgundy leaf twirled around and hit the pane. I clenched my fists, pulled my arms tight to my body, and said to myself, "No more." I may be a refugee now, but I won't be one forever. One day, I will become an American and belong again. Belong somewhere, belong someplace."

I knew English was the ticket out. I had to become fluent so I could bring Behrooz and me to the next level. I almost lost him twice, but by the grace of God I had seen him into America. *America.* We had made it here despite revolution, despite the smugglers, and despite the border-guard ambush that almost killed us. *We—had—made—it—here.*

He needed better. He deserved better, and I was his mother.

As I looked outside, a cardinal landed on a small branch near the window. For a brief moment, we locked eyes. In that moment, just before another leaf fell to the ground, I engaged. I rose, stopped floating, and started slaying the waves again. I dug my feet in the sand and told the current "No!"

◆   ◆   ◆

And so began my journey out. That day, after that bus ride, I motored ahead, kicking the water that slowed me. The shoreline in sight, I lowered my head, spun my arms, and barreled forward.

My first move was to sign up for an "English as a Second Language" class. Every day, Behrooz and I would be at the kitchen table studying our homework. Every spare minute of my time was filled with making flash cards, watching TV, and absorbing language wherever I could. Before I fell asleep at night, words flooded my mind. I hoped this was a sign my brain was making sense of all I had learned that day. English was the way to a better job, a better neighborhood, and a better school for Behrooz. I was obsessed with learning English.

The bad news? I now started to understand what my angry neighbor was yelling to his child. As he raged into the night, I studied my cards and swore I would get out of that apartment before the screen door outside was ever fixed.

Greensburg, Michigan
1980s–2002

This is our purpose:
To make as meaningful as possible this life that has been bestowed upon us …
To live in such a way that we may be proud of ourselves,
To act in such a way that some part of us lives on.

Oswald Spengler

Chapter 25

The days following my decision to get up and out were filled with work at the hotel. The nights were filled with English books. I got a new pair of glasses, thinking that seeing clearly meant understanding clearly. Behrooz was learning English fast and acclimating to life in the United States far better than I had predicted.

Knowing what life was like without a Baba, I was protective of him. Strangely, while he certainly missed Omar and talked freely of him, he did not seem to have the sense of shame I remember having as a child. Then again, he was living in a different country, a separate culture than the one I had known.

After a few years of studying English persistently, I was able to secure a job at a local drugstore. Although the job was a step up, for months after being hired on I was terrified. A large part of my day was spent at the register talking to customers and ringing up items. Some people still spoke too rapidly for me to understand, and at least once every few days I pushed the wrong combination of buttons on the register and had to call the manager for help. Some customers were understanding, but others responded with a puff of air and a hand on their hip. The good thing about prolonged exposure to *anything* is that it desensitizes you. After a few months, customers could whirl their eyes as much as they wanted—it didn't bother me.

Next on the agenda was finding a new place to live. Behrooz was in middle school and about to enter high school. The stakes were getting high, and I wanted him in a safe environment where the teachers actually had the luxury of teaching. I talked to everyone I knew about where to move and how to secure a low-rent apartment.

Ultimately, someone I knew knew someone else who owned an apartment. The apartment was in Strafford, a small university town adjacent to Greensburg. The landlord had been renting the house to college students but soon decided that was more trouble than it was worth. The crowd he had just kicked out had been rowdy and negligent, if not downright destructive. Basically, he was looking for someone who would take pride in the place and not host alcohol-sodden parties.

Behrooz and I fit those criteria. He offered us the apartment, half of a duplex actually, at a reduced rate. The brick house sat on a sweet side street near the university. Primarily a residential area, each season saw homeowners tending to their properties and preparing them for the holidays to come. Christmas brought out crisp lights and bright trees, while spring saw the birth of colorful flowers in the yards and decorative wreaths on people's front doors. Fall was equally lovely, with Halloween and harvest decor in abundance. The lots on our street were small, usually only a quarter of an acre in size. No matter: people made the most of their little plots and nurtured gardens worthy of pause.

The middle and high schools were within walking distance of our home, a fact which put my mind at tremendous ease. The neighborhood was safe, with university students and faculty walking the streets all times of day and night. Behrooz loved his new school. The teachers were kind to him, and the environment fostered learning and growth. Of course, we had regular challenges, but nothing like what had existed in our old neighborhood.

Best of all, we had peaceful neighbors. There were no madmen yelling profanities at their children and no broken doors and windows. People smiled when you passed them on the street, and the most noise you ever heard was when our state university played their rival school during the football season. Unlike in our former neighborhood, however, the police were always quick to arrive and quiet things down.

Those years were busy with work, school, and making a life for ourselves. Behrooz connected with some good friends, and I grew to admire him as he matured and came into his own. He became more like his baba each day, developing a sense of humor and tending to his responsibilities. Before he ever turned sixteen, he was in search of work to help me pay the bills and save for college. He wound up getting a job at a retirement home in the area. He largely worked in the kitchen, a young man working in a sea of old ladies. Against his curly, blue-haired co-workers, his olive skin and raven black hair stood out. He was also about fifty years younger than most of the ladies. In watching him, however, you would never know much of anything separated Behrooz from his "girlfriends." He loved to talk to them, and they loved to be talked to. He was a charmer like his father, and he developed a sense of humor that was all American.

Sometimes when I would get to the home early to pick him up, I would spy on him as he worked. On and on he would go, telling some story I half understood. Only a minute into his tale, the ladies would toss their curly heads back, flash the giggle beneath their necks, and hoot and holler. Cracking only a sliver of a smile himself, Behrooz carried on filling the meal trays for the residents.

My boy was growing up and fitting in. He straddled two worlds. How far he had come. How proud I stood. How much easier I breathed.

Chapter 26

I wanted to get to the auditorium an hour and a half early so I could be sure to get a seat as close to the students as possible. I hadn't bought new clothes in about two years until this occasion, which warranted an investment. On a half-off rack at the mall I had found a pale blue suit and a pair of black patent leather shoes. I bought them without an ounce of guilt. My baby was graduating from high school, and I was his mother.

The ceremony was set for five PM, and I double-checked my camera three times to make sure the film was working. It was a hot day, and no matter how much goop I smoothed onto my frizzy hair, it puffed up in resistance. I finally gave up and pinned it back. As I came out of my bedroom, I saw Behrooz looking out the window. He too had a new suit. It was navy blue and accented by a red tie. His glasses were shiny clean, and whatever he had put in his hair had served him well. His waves scooped around his scalp and ever so gently found rest on his shirt collar.

"Well," he said. "Can you believe this?"

I told myself I wouldn't let him see me cry, but within a second I could feel my chin quiver and tears cloud my eyes. I rushed over to hug him. "It's okay, Maman," he said. "It's okay."

From there we headed to the school. I found a seat up high where I could see him walk in. An hour later, the commencement music started. I searched for the boy who would always be a part of me. Child after child entered until I finally saw the raven hair I knew so well. He tilted his head up toward the balcony, and I waved as if I hadn't seen him in years. He was "cool" in his gesture back, but as I watched him vigorously scan the crowd for me, I realized I was still safely anchored in his life.

As I watched him receive his diploma and walk across the stage, I clenched my fists and felt my chest fill with emotion. The woman beside me was also a graduate's mother, but she sat so calmly, so composed. I felt embarrassed by my tears, but then I thought about the goat that got us giggling in Baluchistan, the hours we had sat studying English at the kitchen table, and that hospital room in Pakistan. The ruby-nosed nurse's face flashed in my mind, and then I remembered those bejeweled buses that looked so silly fumbling their way down the streets. I saw Behrooz at ten years old, still limping from the accident, pointing and laughing at the silver and gold beads flapping against the sides of the bus. I also saw him as an awkward teenager and then a young man, completely adept at negotiating two cultures. I thought of him handing me his paycheck each week, and never complaining about what we couldn't afford. I felt his hand on my shoulder after a long day at work, and I heard his voice translating words I couldn't understand as I stood in a government office only months in country. I was supposed to be taking care of him then, but it certainly felt otherwise.

It was then I knew I deserved to cry. I was entitled to every emotion that came to me in that moment.

Chapter 27

In 2001 Second Chances was still resettling refugees down the street from me. I rarely visited the office any more, but I kept in limited contact with some of its employees. Thanks to these connections, I was offered a new job.

The Taliban had taken over Afghanistan in 1996 and succeeded in turning back time for women. Strict Islamic law had been imposed, and archaic practices were in full force. Women were forbidden to work, and girls were banned from attending school and leaving their homes alone. As if that were not enough, the level of violence had escalated to such a degree that parents were even afraid to send their *boys* to school. An entire generation of children was in jeopardy of becoming illiterate.

How ironic: literate parents raising illiterate children.

In any event, by 2001 the United States had started resettling larger numbers of refugees from Afghanistan. These refugees were generally widowed women with children, the disabled, and victims of torture. By 2001, Afghanistan had been a nation at risk for decades. In fact, the United States had been resettling Afghans since the Soviet invasion in 1979. My friend at sewing circle, Aneesa, the diplomat's wife, had been one of them. Sadly, Afghanistan had continued to decline since that time. As a result, millions of Afghans had either been killed or made into refugees.

Greensburg was one of the towns that had agreed to resettle a fraction of the Afghan population. That's where I came in. Afghan families were coming to Greensburg, and Second Chances needed an interpreter. By 2001 I had learned English and interviewed for the position. I was offered the job and quit the pharmacy the next day.

My first office job, I thought. I would have a desk and a phone, and I would be able to sit down while I worked. Adrenaline—*the good kind*—pulsed through my body.

◆   ◆   ◆

While I had worked strenuous jobs before, interpreting was a new kind of strenuous. Finally able to relax after all these years, my body rested in an office chair as I worked. My mind, however, might as well have been climbing sand-covered dunes each day.

First off, I had to listen to *every* word a client said. This wasn't always a challenge, but I admit that a verbose client who droned on and on sometimes sent my mind dreaming.

Next, I had to search my brain for the *exact* word my client had used. Some words are easy, but other words represent concepts that only exist in one language. When they have an important cultural meaning attached to them, there really is no foreign equivalent. When such a word or phrase presented itself, all I could do was explain the *message* someone was trying to get across.

Serious examples exist, but here is a funny one. A Farsi proverb says that a hostess is the donkey of her guests. That means one should extend the utmost hospitality to one's invited company. I have known friends, however, who have literally translated this proverb, and all the hostess heard was that she was a donkey.

Other confusion arises from distinctly Persian customs such as *taruf,* which involves declining an invitation upon first request. For example, if you ask a Persian to go somewhere, eat something, and so on, a polite person will always say "no" at first. You should then ask again, insist perhaps a third time, and then, if he really wants to eat or go somewhere, you'll know the answer on the third or fourth try. The lesson? Never take the first reply as definitive because it will always be "no." That is *taruf,* that is what is polite.

So, some translation requires far more explanation and cultural context than others.

Then there are the dialects and accents. While Iranians and Dari speaking Afghans speak the same language, we pronounce words differently and even use separate words from time to time. I was not familiar with Dari, the Farsi spoken in Afghanistan, and so at times I struggled to understand what a person was saying. In fact, when some Afghan groups spoke among themselves, I could not understand them at all. I am sure the same can be said of we Iranians.

Finally, there is the flipping back and forth. During my first week as an interpreter, I felt like someone was slapping me on one cheek and then, just as I turned my face in that direction, I would get slapped on the opposite cheek. Back and forth my head went. *Slap, slap.* I felt frazzled and depleted. At night, before I fell asleep, words in both languages swarmed my mind. The mechanics of interpreting wore me down.

I can't talk about translating, however, without making mention of the psychological side of it. In a few weeks I got used to the technical aspects of my job and can now flip languages as easily as putting on or taking off a coat. English coat, *okay.* Farsi, *no problem.* I have even learned to translate those words that travel with a cultural message.

It is the *psychological* toll, however, that I still pay.

◆   ◆   ◆

"How are your children?" a caseworker asked the Afghan woman beside me.

"Good."

"How do they like school?" he continued.

"They like it," she told me. I translated her words.

"Good. Well, you have been at Peterson's eight months now. Good for you." Peterson's was a local company many of the Sewing Circle women moved into when their skills improved and they sought employment. "Okay, well...." The caseworker signed some papers in his file and then closed its pale yellow cover. As I watched him put the file into a metal bin, I saw tears spring from the woman's eyes.

Like the Shoua of my past, I placed my hand on the woman's forearm.

"*What's wrong?* I thought everything was going well!" the caseworker said, somewhat alarmed and definitely surprised.

The woman, who had been originally facing the caseworker, pivoted around and sat directly across from me. I was only supposed to be a vehicle through which she was to communicate with the caseworker. A sort of nonentity, or faceless voice anyway. With this pivot, my role changed. The caseworker became secondary.

"I have all these bills. Look at this electricity bill, and then the bill for our airfare." She fanned papers at me. "I have five children, and I am the only one working. I make five-twenty-five an hour. I will *never* get these bills paid. My arms and shoulders are tired from bending over the sewing machines, and my eyes twitch."

I tried to interpret as fast as I could to keep the caseworker in the loop. The woman didn't care if he followed or not, she just kept talking.

"The nights are the worst. I am tired, yet I can't sleep. It is like my mind is running movies."

"Movies?" I asked.

"Yes, the same film all the time. It usually happens just before I fall asleep or while I am winding down. Suddenly, I'm back in Afghanistan. I am in the kitchen, making *nan*, when I hear commotion outside. I look out the window, being careful not to let anyone see me from behind the curtain."

At this point, I stopped translating and decided to listen to the balance of her story. I would fill the caseworker in at the end.

"As I look out," she continued, "I see it is a Talib. A Talib with a long beard. Soon, a pickup truck arrives. Taliban clamber out of the bed of the truck. They are slinging guns around their young, bony bodies.

"I turn away from the window. My heart bangs with life. With fear. I hear screams, screams from a woman, my neighbor. She just had a baby a month ago. I know her screams."

Scream.

Scream.

Bang.

Bang.

Silence.

The roar of an engine.

Silence.

A baby's shriek.

As she spoke, her shaking hands worked to dry the tears on her face. After a minute or two, she gave up and let them comb her cheeks and neck.

It was the last bit of the story—the child's wail—that started my tears. I had been holding them back for minutes, but it was then my restraint failed me. With a simple word, the vision of a motherless child, I surrendered. Tears filled my eyes and leaked out.

When she saw my eyes water, her back buckled, and she pulled her arms underneath her chest. She was in a near fetal position as she sat on the wooden chair.

"Meetra Jon"—a term of endearment—"I did nothing. *Nothing.*"

I closed my eyes. Her words stung me.

"I didn't go outside in protest. I didn't call anyone for help. My own brother was in the other room. He is big and tall—the protective type. I didn't even tell him what I had just seen. I didn't look out the window again. I didn't move the curtain. I just stood there. *I did nothing.*"

She and I had been holding hands for a few minutes. I then took my remaining hand and placed it over hers. Her small, callused fingers sandwiched between my palms.

"Meetra, I did nothing. I left Afghanistan. That is what I did." She then bowed her head in complete and all-consuming shame.

With that, I embraced her. The caseworker looked at me and waited. All I needed to say was "Taliban," and he knew. No need to go into the details. He took a deep breath, rubbed his hand across his tired forehead, and closed his eyes wearisomely.

◆   ◆   ◆

That day transported me back to the 1980s and my own shame at not having stood up. I too had walked away. There are few heroes in this life, and the problem was that I was confused by who they were. Should that poor woman have taken on the Taliban outside her door? Sacrificed her brother? Possibly left her own children orphaned?

The simple answer is "no." But then, if no one ever protests, how do we progress? Change? Become better? What risks are worth taking and which ones are futile? Which are a waste of time, a waste of a life?

The old questions came flooding back to me almost twenty years after I had made my own decision to escape. I had chosen to get out and away.

As I merged onto the expressway and headed toward my apartment, my mind traveled back. How depleting and debilitating shame can be. From one side of the globe to the other, no matter what war-torn country we came from, we all knew that one action, one random moment, could change everything. Everything could come to an end.

Despite knowing this, we tried to subsist. We moved gingerly, one step after the other, living with the guilt of not measuring up to our own expectations of ourselves. We all dreamed our lives would be different. We all wanted to be heroes, to act nobly, and yet many of us felt as though we had stepped aside. When all was said and done, we lived with and resented this stark, poignant truth every day.

◆   ◆   ◆

And so, I ached for the families I worked with, and when I was finished interpreting for them, I wondered what I should say or do. Usually, I just let them cry and talk about their struggles. I held their hands and told them that I admired their strength and courage. I told them that although it might be impossible to see now, these were the toughest years. The first five were the most agonizing, but it went up from there. I talked about Behrooz, and then I said this: "You are here for your children. *Their future.* They will make a life in this country."

Whenever I said this, tears sprung to my eyes as though the words were new to me. Once uttered, however, the women always paused, blinked, and nodded their head.

"Yes."

They would always say "yes," and then they would say no more.

Chapter 28

My work at Second Chances largely circled around the Afghan population, but of course I came to know and meet people from all over the world. Most of the people who worked at the agency were foreign, and many were former refugees themselves. Each day, those of us eating in for lunch congregated in the small kitchen in the basement. One day, I remember a lively exchange as several of us hunted through the refrigerator for our afternoon meals.

"Oh, that smells good," a Cuban woman said as a Kurdish lady put her dish into the microwave and the scent of garlic and tomatoes filled the air.

"*Bomieh*. Okra!" the Kurdish woman said.

The Cuban woman then put her rice and beans into the microwave. I fetched a plate for the feta cheese I regularly stuffed into some pita with a few sprigs of fresh mint. A Persian classic.

"What do you have today, Ameena?" Ameena was a Somalian woman who also worked with us.

"Sambusas!" she said.

"My favorite," I replied. Sambusas are like Somalian egg rolls, fried pockets containing a delicious stuffing. They are typically triangular, but Ameena made hers into cylinders because she said it was easier. For the most part, the Somalians fill their sambusas with vegetables, ground meat, and a bit of curry. I absolutely love them.

Once we had all warmed and prepared our meals, we immediately started filling each other's plates. Just as I turned to offer Ameena some of the fresh fruit and feta cheese I had brought, I watched a sambusa roll across my plate and slam into a heaping mound of Cuban rice. With only a few seconds to catch its breath, the sambusa was then crowded in by little pieces of okra in a tomato-garlic sauce. My sambusa was surrounded from all corners, and I had not even had a chance to put my own food onto my plate yet!

Yes, I soon learned, when you dined in, you brought plenty to share.

"You know, we are having a party next week," the Cuban woman said, scooping some rice onto her spoon.

"Oh great—I love the parties we have here. So lively, so much fun," I said. "What are you going to bring?" I asked.

"I don't know. I would like to bring a pork roast. My family has a wonderful recipe for an orange sauce, but I know some people don't eat pork."

"Yes, I don't eat pork." The Kurdish woman said.

"Me either," said the Somalian woman.

"Perhaps the old stand-by. Black beans and rice then. What about you guys?"

"I was thinking about a bryani," said the Kurdish woman.

"What's that?"

"It is a rice dish that has chicken, potatoes, and raisins. Very good!"

"I don't understand," Ameena said. "Why are you talking about what to bring?"

"It's a potluck party," the Cuban woman said.

"What's that?"

"It means that we each bring a dish to share—'to pass' as they say in America."

"We are supposed to *cook ourselves!*" the Somalian woman said, her fork freezing in mid-air and her eyebrows raising in surprise. I smirked and lowered my head. I understood the confusion.

"It's quite customary in this country. People have parties like this all the time. Is it strange to you?" the Cuban woman said.

"It's like saying, 'You can come over to visit, but you have to bring your own food!'"

With that I started to laugh and thought about all the times I spent ridiculous amounts of money, not to mention days in the kitchen, preparing for parties in Iran. Like in Somalia, in Iran you never asked your guests to show up with food for the party. That would have been a high-order insult!

"Well, I guess it is kind of like asking people to bring their own food, but it is actually much easier to entertain when it is potluck. A lot less work."

With that the Somalian woman tilted her head, lowered her eyes, and said—obviously without buying in, "If you say so!" Then she asked, "What does 'potluck' mean anyway?"

We looked at each another and shrugged. No one knew.

Over the months I not only sampled delicious home-cooked meals from all over the world, but I also laughed with my colleagues and gradually became friends with them. I continued to learn not only about America but about countries I knew I would never visit.

In that vein, I'll always remember my first taste of Cuban coffee. My friend Pedro, a refugee from the island, had some stored in a Coke bottle in the refrigerator. After all the rice I had eaten that afternoon, I was ready for a siesta. He went to the refrigerator, pulled the plastic bottle from the shelf, poured the heavy coffee into a lovely china cup, and warmed it in the microwave. He brought it to me, and I worked for four hours straight. It was the strongest beverage I had ever had, but with the sugar helping to round out the bitterness of the coffee beans, I actually developed an affinity for the little cup that packed so much punch. It was delicious, so whenever the rice got to me, I hit Pedro up for some coffee. Of course, I was sure to bring some cardamom cake for us to share too. After all, we both came from cultures where generosity was prized, and making others feel welcome and appreciated, especially with food, was customary.

◆   ◆   ◆

My job at Second Chances involved picking up "new arrivals" at the airport, taking them to their apartments, and interpreting for their caseworkers. That meant I traveled back and forth to my old neighborhood frequently, which was one of the places new arrivals were assigned to live. I now had a driver's license, and as I would pull into the parking lot of my old complex, I would dodge the shopping carts that reminded me of snowy days and teary trips to the market. Asked where the local grocery store was, I could always give the newcomers precise directions.

In addition to the official duties associated with my position, my work with the Afghans extended into other areas. We shared both a common language and the experience of being ejected by our homelands. Yet something else, something special and intangible, endeared me to the families I worked with. Some of it had to do with coming to appreciate what over twenty years of war had done to this nation. Everyone I met had lost loved ones, and all had stories of what the mujahideen and the Taliban had done to their homes and families. The women I worked with shed thousands of tears in my years at the agency, and I came to have a tremendous empathy for the roads they had traveled and the losses they had endured.

I also have to say that I found Afghans the most generous and giving people I have ever met. A single mother of five could be living on four hundred dollars a month and still find a way to make *nan-e-khosht*, bread, for me on my way out the door. I never left an Afghan home without a meal, tea and cakes, or food for the road. Often, I would leave with a steaming pot of rice or bag of fruit they had just purchased at the market. I felt guilty taking hard-earned food from them, but they always insisted.

And when there was no food to offer, they found other ways to express their appreciation.

◆   ◆   ◆

"Thank you, Meetra Jon. Thank you for helping Farida with her homework."

"My pleasure. She is learning more and more each week." As I looked down at the second grader, I gave her a wink, and she beamed a smile.

"When are you coming back *Khaleh Jon*, dear aunt?" All the Afghan children called me *Khaleh*, and when I first heard the term and witnessed its wide use, I thought back to the days of my youth. Back then, "khaleh" conjured up images of bird's nest hairdos and tunes filling the air.

"I'll see you the day after tomorrow. Now remember, work on your flashcards," I said with an encouraging smile and a pat on her shoulder.

"Oh Meetra, thank you so much. *Zendeh Basheed.*" A blessing of sorts. "But you didn't eat anything! You're too skinny. You should eat something."

Both she and I knew that there wasn't much in the house to offer up. I had sipped some tea and munched on some raisins while we did math problems earlier, but that was all I had eaten.

"Oh, thank you, but I am not hungry. I have to get home anyway."

With that, I leaned down to put on my shoes. Just as I had pulled the lace through the knot and was on my way back up, I felt a spray hit my neck. A second later, I smelled the faint scent of flowers crowded out by the stronger smell of alcohol.

Farida's mother was smiling and holding a perfume bottle in her right hand. I could tell from the looks of the glass and the smell of its contents that the bottle had traveled far. Probably it had been saved for years—closely guarded and brought out only on special occasions.

"Thank you!" I said. "It smells lovely. You should save it, not waste it on me."

"You are helping Farida so much. I want you to know how much I appreciate it."

Alternating cheeks, I kissed her three times, once more than we Iranians customarily do. "You are kind, thank you. I look forward to seeing you soon. "And you," I added, looking down at Farida. "You take care." I reached down for kisses number four, five, and six.

With that, I was out the door, trailed by the perfume that had been carried from Afghanistan to Pakistan and then to America. The perfume that harkened back to better times. The bottle that was all that was left of home.

◆   ◆   ◆

As the calendar pages flipped, fall came along with Halloween. Costumes were out of the question for most families on a tight budget. I found myself at our local twenty-four-hour supermarket at four in the morning on Halloween day. Bleary-eyed, I pulled at the racks, searching for half-priced outfits. Because I had been fortunate enough to find housing in a neighborhood conducive to trick-or-treating, I tried to invite a few families each year to our block in search of candy. I lived in an area with scores of children where it was safe for little ones to travel about.

Then came Thanksgiving, which is my absolute favorite holiday. First, it is a secular holiday, an American holiday, with no opportunity for people to feel left out for religious or ethnic reasons. More to the point, it is a day to offer thanks and talk about what we are grateful for. That's certainly something we refugees know something about.

Of course, most of the Afghans I worked with knew little of Thanksgiving. I guessed it would be a good holiday to celebrate together. I hoped that by inviting them to my home I could help them feel a little more a part of our country. Too, I was tired of hearing Americans say that immigrants never wanted to participate in American traditions and customs. After all, you have to be introduced, sometimes asked, to participate and learn about new traditions. Yes, most refugees didn't celebrate Thanksgiving when they first came—but they had no idea what it was about. No one had shown them what to do!

So in 2001, my first annual Thanksgiving celebration started. That year I invited two families to dinner. My apartment was small, but no one seemed to notice. I bought a turkey at the grocery store and, after some good advice from an American friend, made sure it was thawed by Thursday. And yes, I also remembered to take out the giblets; plastic-wrapped organs on our plate was not one of the traditions I wanted to take hold.

A few years back, Behrooz, had convinced me in one of my weak moments to buy a TV dish so we could have a greater selection of channels. One day, scrolling through the excessive listings and wondering why I had given in, I happened upon the cooking channel: the Food Network. Day after day, whenever I had the time, I would tune in to see what was literally cooking. It was better than watching the news—certainly less depressing—and it was informative. I was learning about meals I could make in less than thirty minutes or meals with an Italian flair. There were even themed weeks when a particular set of recipes were shared with the TV viewing audience.

The week before Thanksgiving, several detailed shows taught viewers how to prepare a turkey and traditional American side dishes to serve with it. As I sat there with a dish of Persian stew on my lap, I watched and took notes. By the time Thanksgiving rolled around, I had decided to make mashed potatoes, green beans, and a few pies. The pies were the hardest of all. So much time for one little dish of dough and fruit. After that first year, I never made them again.

On Thanksgiving Day, my guests arrived. Because the holiday fell over Ramadan, the Islamic fast, we waited until sundown to feast. After *Namaz,* prayer, we broke out the food. For the first time that night, everyone was quiet. We were all starved.

Just as everyone was heading for seconds, I spoke up. "I know earlier we talked about the history of Thanksgiving, but I wanted to share a custom with you I learned about a number of years ago. When I first came to this country, Behrooz and I were invited to an American family's house. There, before we ate, we went around the table and talked about what we were grateful for. I thought it was a lovely tradition. Perhaps we might try it tonight?"

"Yes, very good idea," one of the women said.

"How about we start with you, *Kaw-Kaw,* uncle?" said another. This was another affectionate term like aunt, used to address men in a respectful manner.

The older man, my friend's father, bowed his head and touched his hand to his chest, signifying thanks and respect. "I want to thank you for inviting us to your home today. For all the cooking you did, and for making us feel so welcome. You have helped...."

He spoke at length about what he thought I had done for his family, and I shook my head, denying that I had done much of anything to move them forward. He disagreed and continued complimenting me. Appreciative of his gesture, I knew that the family had fared well because of its strength, tenacity, and commitment to one another. As is usual with the Afghans, however, he rejected my reverse flattery and continued on even more graciously and appreciatively than was necessary or true. They had made it on their own. This I knew.

Then it was time for one of the children to speak. The little girl who sat to the right of *Kaw-Kaw* was about nine years old. Before coming to the United States she had never attended school.

"I am grateful for my school. Oh, and my teacher who is so nice to me."

The next child carried on. "I am grateful for school, too. Especially for the new pencils and paper."

"I am grateful for the bus that comes and takes me to school," the next child said. "If there were no bus, I could not get there."

"I am grateful we don't have to pay money to go to school. If we did, I wouldn't be able to go," another offered up.

The youngest child was last. "I am grateful for my mommy," the littlest one said. The table erupted in laughter while his mother reached over and kissed his turkey-packed cheek.

Next it was time for one of the mothers to speak. A woman who had become a close and cherished friend to me began. As she placed her fork down and looked around the table, she breathed deeply. "I am grateful for my children and for your friendship." She reached out and touched my hand. "I am grateful to be healthy and to see my children in school and learning."

Her voice started to quiver. She took her hand, braced by her thumb and middle finger, and clasped her temples. She continued, eyes humbly shielded. "I am grateful to the United States. America took my family in when no one else wanted us. I am grateful I can work in this country and that my children can become educated." Here, she was obviously referring to the sad reality so many refugees face. Often, they are denied work and school in the countries they first escape into, the countries they flee to for safety and protection. We all knew America was different in this regard. Not only could our children go to school, *it was the law.* Not only could we work, we were *expected* to so we could rebuild our lives. We were grateful for such laws—such opportunities.

Then she continued. "I am grateful for peace." With this, the tears rolled. "I am grateful not to hear rockets booming in the night, and I am grateful for not having to worry about the mines my children might step on. Finally, I am grateful for the chance to become a citizen of this country. *I will do it!*"

She then looked at her two teenaged children who had been tutoring her on her citizen test questions. They, on her coattails, would also become citizens if she passed the exam. They all studied together, eyes on the prize.

In finishing, she said, "This is a wonderful holiday. This Thanksgiving. I am just so grateful. So very grateful for everything."

By that point, everyone in the room was wiping tears of grace, exhaustion, and mutual sentiment from their eyes.

It was then I knew we had celebrated. We had embraced Thanksgiving.

◆　　◆　　◆

So, I happily engaged in "mission creep" while working at Second Chances. Lest it sound like an exasperating experience altogether, there were times, of course, that I just plain howled out loud in laughter.

Raman was Arab and stood about eye level with me. I am five feet two inches tall. He was rounded across his middle, and when he leaned back on his office chair to tell a story, his feet lifted off the ground.

Raman and I worked together on a lot of cases. One sunny April day we showed up to take a client to an appointment. Dressed professionally, files in hand, we climbed the stairs of the client's complex and knocked on the door.

A minute or so passed. Just when we were about to knock again, the door opened and a shocked face appeared.

"Hello, we are from Second Chances," I said.

"Hello, please come in," a man in his mid-twenties said. As we entered the apartment, a woman tottered in from the other room. She was carrying a tray of tea and dried fruit. "Please," she said as she put the tray on the coffee table and gestured for us to eat. She was about seventy-five and spoke no English.

In the background I heard a lot of noise coming from the TV, but I ignored the sounds. I have never been one to notice details. As I looked at Raman, however, I caught him gawking at the television.

"What are you watching, man?" Raman asked.

"I don't know, man, I am trying to figure this out!" he said. By then, I had focused in. Amid all the yelling and gibberish coming from the set were beeping sounds. In fact, I couldn't make out what the people were saying either. One, they were yelling, two, the audience was screaming, and three, there were constant, high-pitched sounds overpowering the dialogue. When I finally did focus on the picture instead of the sounds, I saw a woman peel off her clothes and reveal herself to be a man.

There we stood—Raman, the client, his bowlegged mother, and me. We were all lined up in front of the screen, jaws open, eyes transfixed. Raman was the first to cover his mouth, gasp, and wag his index finger at the set.

"Oh, no. No. This is not good, man!" His finger kept swinging from left to right and then back again. I didn't understand what was going on. It seemed like every other word was a beep. Now the people on the screen had gotten up out of their chairs and were flailing their arms and screaming. The audience was hooting and hollering, and then someone threw a chair.

"America?" the man asked, pointing to the screen and looking at us.

The grandmother, who had now added her wagging finger to Raman's, limped over to the TV and turned the channel to a soap opera. She then collapsed onto the couch and started to tell us all about the story unfolding on the screen. Without a lick of English under her belt, she knew who loved whom, who was conceived out of wedlock, and who was about to be murdered. Once done with the saga, she popped an almond into her mouth and motioned Raman to move away from the screen. He was blocking her view.

Nothing to say, we left the apartment, all wondering about this America we had just witnessed. On our way to the appointment Raman periodically shook his head and said, "*Oh no. Not good. Not good at all.*" His short body was only inches from the steering wheel, and as he straightened his chubby leg and pressed the accelerator, his index finger, perched atop the wheel, started to wag again. "*No. No. Not good,*" he muttered to himself, shaking his head in disbelief.

"America?" the refugee asked again. Neither of us knew what to say.

◆   ◆   ◆

Then there was the "cultural whiplash," as I liked to call it. I largely worked with Afghans and other Middle Easterners with whose culture I was familiar. For example, I knew that when it came to men I was to be reserved. In fact, for the most part, I knew to restrain myself from any physical gestures, sometimes including handshakes, depending on the culture of the family. I also knew that as a woman I was expected to be soft-spoken and not talk too much.

With this understanding as a backdrop, one day I came into the office only to have Raman send me back out to pick up two Cubans. They had various appointments that day. Their address was scribbled on a ripped piece of paper, and when I reached the apartment, the two were waiting outside for me. As I pulled the car into the driveway, put it into park, and unlocked the doors, one of the men, like a shot, jumped right into the front seat. The other eased into the back. I was immediately thrown and a bit chagrined. No Middle Eastern man I would have picked up would have come into the front without asking, and many would have just sat in the back.

Once he pulled the door shut, he looked directly in my eyes and started talking. His English was good, better than his buddy's in the back, and so we proceeded to converse for the next four hours straight.

Alexander talked about his life in Cuba and the limits of living in a communist society. He had originally come to Florida but wound up homeless for six months. Then he heard about Second Chances. He was in search of work and a woman. That's right—he wanted a wife, and he went on for hours about her.

He also liked the ladies in general, as I soon came to find out one day in the parking lot. Crossing from the street to the sidewalk was a tall woman with long, chestnut brown hair. As she searched her overstuffed bag, her hair fell across her face, allowing the sun to reveal the highlights lining her mane. She was dressed in pumps, a gray skirt, and a bright blue blazer. No sooner had she stepped foot onto the pavement than I heard ol' Alex yelling, "*Hey* pretty lady!"

Not used to correcting men and not sure if it was even a good idea, I did anyway.

"Hey Alex, in America we don't usually yell out compliments like that."

"What? Women like to know they're pretty, don't they? No harm in offering up some praise!"

"No, but this is not the way we generally do it."

"Ah! *Hi* pretty lady!" he said again, twisting his head like an owl.

At that point, I just tugged on his jacket and guided him into the building.

Hours later, I pulled my car into the lot at Second Chances, happy to hear nothing but the hum of my engine. As I got out of the driver's seat, went into the building, and climbed the stairs of the agency, I started to shake my head in laughter. By the time I had gotten to Raman's office, I was swinging my bag, giddy. I couldn't keep the smirk off my face as I pushed open the glass door.

"Hey," he said. "How did it go?" As he greeted me, he folded his hands behind his head and leaned back in his chair. His feet dangled in the air, and he crossed his legs, hoping, I guess, to give them some support.

"Whiplash," I said.

"What?"

"Cultural whiplash," I said, falling into the chair across from him and laying the back of my hand against my forehead. I was mocking my own drama.

"Ah, yeah. You were with the Cubans today." He was clueing in.

"Raman, you can't send me out with Moslem men in the morning and Cuban men in the afternoon. It'll kill me!"

With that, we laughed, knowing neither of us meant any harm or disrespect to either population. Cultures vary, and it was as simple and as complex as that.

Greensburg, Michigan
2005

I cannot believe that the purpose of life is to be happy. I think the purpose of life is to be useful, to be responsible, to be compassionate. It is, above all to matter, to count, to stand for something, to have made some difference that you lived at all.

Leo Rosten

Chapter 29

Dear Maman,

I should call you about this news, but there is so much I want to say. So much I should have told you before today that I have not.

First things first. You will soon be the grandmother of a baby girl! We have decided to name her Azadeh. A name meaning "freedom" seems so perfect—so fitting. She will come to us in July, so be sure to put in for all the vacation you can get.

Even though this news is enough to fill a letter, the other reason I needed to write is to tell you what I should have told you years ago.

Maman, I need to thank you. I always knew you were strong enough to take care of us, but I didn't realize how hard it was to be this strong. I remember thinking how tired your dark eyes looked as you put me to bed at night. What I didn't understand is how tired you were on the inside.

Sometimes I felt you loved me too hard, too closely. My American friends had more freedom, more latitude to make choices and live parallel to their parents. On my worst days, I felt envious. Now, as a man, as someone who is soon to be a father, life has a nuance it never had.

Yesterday a man from Mexico brought his daughter into the emergency room with a laceration to the head. She was going be fine, but his eyes kept filling with tears and he paced the room as we worked. I tried reassuring him, but then he gripped my forearm and said: "Doctor, you don't understand. It has just been the two of us since she was one. Her mother died of cancer, and I am the one who must see her out of childhood. I work two jobs to keep her fed and clothed, and I don't have any insurance. She deserves the same care any child does, but I can't help her without your helping me. I can't go back to Mexico. I love this country, and I speak English. I want to work so she will have a better life than me. She *has* to make it."

My eyes filled too as I listened to his words. When he was finished, I placed my hand on top of his and said, "She will make it." I then told him our

157

story—yours and mine—and he bowed his head, covered his face with his dark weathered hands, and buckled in tears.

Maman, I would not be here if it were not for you. Your courage, your grit, your compassion, turned us into survivors.

Rest easy, Maman. You did all you needed to do.

I love you,
Behrooz

Chapter 30

Well, we are about at the end of our time together. What can I say?

I consider it a privilege to still be working at Second Chances. My direct work with Afghan refugees has diminished some since 9/11 and the toppling of the Taliban. Some refugees still trickle in, but not the numbers that did years ago.

It has been an honor to watch the women I've known rise and strengthen. I have witnessed illiterate mothers raise valedictorian children. I've seen women who were victims of torture and trauma find their smiles again.

Like all families—like me—they have their setbacks. Still, they cleave together, fixated on making a life here. Actively and passively, they have accepted that this is their home now. In fact, I have yet to meet a refugee who wants to go back.

They worry about relatives at "home," and they worry about the bills. They are fighting to get out of the "bad" neighborhoods, and they drive their children to study hard and go to college.

We talk about these things over Thanksgiving dinners and in the Sewing Circle I am still a part of. Yes, over twenty years later I find myself sitting around that same table talking about the events of our world and how they impact us. This time, I am the interpreter telling the stories of the Afghan women I sit with. There are others too. Now Somalian, Sudanese, Liberian, and Kurdish women sew and talk with us as well. I find myself curious about those sitting beside me. I wonder what happened to them—really happened to them—that put them in danger. I don't ask, but most of the time I get some sense of what they experienced when they share some detail, some story, that helps me fill in the blanks. That said, I know it is never the full story—never the darkest side of the tale. Most of us don't want to *think* about all that happened to us, let alone *talk* about what we witnessed. I guess in the end I am the same way. When people ask me about Omar or Irandokht, I offer up a prepared answer that is vague and yet complete. I answer in a tone of voice that sends the message, "Don't ask me anything more. Stop." Most people then change the subject. I've never shared the real details with anyone, not even Behrooz when he asked. For better or worse, I will leave this world knowing things others do not. My deepest horrors will stay hidden.

Occasionally, out of nowhere I hear a *"salaam!"* uttered in such a way that I know the woman can't be anything but Iranian.

Because I have spent so much time with Afghans over the past number of years, I speak more Dari than Farsi. Sometimes, people even think I am Afghan instead of Iranian. When I do meet a Persian woman though, a woman who is a refugee for many of the same reasons I am one, there is an immediate ease between us. We look into one another's eyes and see ourselves, our children, and those we have lost. We see our mamans with their shaking cooking spoons and our babas who lifted us up to the sky. We see our great nation, our proud culture, and we wonder if we will ever be able to go back—or forward, one might say—and see it again. With no answers forthcoming, we usually then weep and share a sympathetic hug shortly after our first "hello's."

Sadly, I can't help but think about how little has changed since I came to America. We still live in a world where governments betray their people, where the innocent are tortured and killed. Listening to what goes on in Africa, the Middle East, and other parts of the globe wears on me. As I said before, interpreting forces you not only to listen to stories but to repeat them. I have had to expand my vocabulary to include words like rape, behead, abuse, drug, and stab so that I can tell the stories of those with whom I sit and sew each week.

What we do to one another in this world, I will never understand.

Chapter 31

Today I am sitting on the beach, watching the ocean waves lick my toes. The sun came up hours ago, but the beach is still relatively empty. Rest assured, it will soon fill up with all those people determined to get in the last few breaths of summer. School will be starting, and the rhythm of life will change.

As I look out across the Atlantic Ocean, I feel swallowed by the horizon. It is long, and it is far. I think back to my own life and wonder what lies on the other side of that straight line.

My life has traversed over half a century and half a globe. I have lost family, and I have witnessed new branches of this same family grow. Behrooz now lives on the East Coast and has just bought a home on Long Beach Island. Eighteen miles of shoreline grace this little island, and in special places one can see both the ocean and bay at once. Two grand bodies of water simultaneously.

The one bridge on and off the island swarms with people Memorial Day through Labor Day, but the rest of the year is still, leaving much space for thought and reflection. The large red and white lighthouse at the tail of the island is called Barnegat Light. I love to head north, take Long Beach Boulevard as far as it will go, turn left at the street light, and veer toward the lighthouse. It sits on the end of the island where it is hard to tell where the bay ends and the ocean begins. There are quiet places to sit and think, and there are nooks you can escape into and feel all alone. The *good* kind of alone.

In the summer, a soft breeze wipes away the season's heat, and in the winter the breeze turns hard and whips all who enter its path. Those who watch the sea know it likes to change its face. I never tire of searching the waters for an expression I have yet to see.

Behrooz is now grown and has a family himself. He wants me to move to the coast, but I am not ready. I have important work yet to do.

The world is full of refugees. Almost twelve million strong in 2005. This number, of course, does not even start to count those who are internally displaced or those who are warehoused in refugee camps, prisons in themselves.

There is much to be done.

Chapter 32

A few years ago I got into the habit of listening to National Public Radio. A colleague at work introduced me to the station, and I now whittle away the hours listening to various programs available throughout the day.

The station has been running a series called, "This I Believe." Here, NPR invites listeners to write essays addressing what it is *they* believe. I have listened attentively for weeks, dazzled and awestruck by the personal professions of truth.

After listening to today's essay, something deep within me moved—something that needed to find voice.

I got on my bicycle, stuffed a pad of paper into the front basket, and made my way to a small local park beside the bay. Off to the side was a playground and gazebo. By the water's edge, a long dock sprang forward into the water. From the shoreline you could see the causeway, the bridge linking the island to the mainland. Cars zipped across, but because of their distance, the air was silent.

I took my notepad and small beach chair and went out to the end of the dock. There was barely anyone around, and those who were wanted to keep to themselves. We smiled to one another but left each other to our thoughts and reflections.

Soon, I found myself alone with a seagull who flew overhead. Once tired, he rested his body on the dock piling. He would look at me, and I would look at him, but like the people in the park, we left it at that. As the sun shone overhead and the tall grass in the shallow water bent to the soft breeze, I started to write.

I had always wanted to write, but life had taken over. Survival had reigned. Too, I knew that writing about my life required distance, hindsight. *Wisdom.*

As I sat there, I scribbled down words and phrases. After a while I looked up to see if the seagull was still there. While I had written in fury, he had taken flight and was now settling himself between two bright, shimmering waves in the bay. He was facing north and eyeing the sailboat cutting across the crisp water.

I looked back down at my pad and thought about my life. My son was now raised, and I was blessed with a granddaughter and a job that gave me a sense of purpose. I was in a place in my life where I was granted the room to reflect and the room to create. I started to write again, and the seagull came back, perching himself on the piling to my right. His shadow covered the edge of my pad.

As I sat there, here is what came to me.

This I Believe.

I believe in never underestimating the power of an instant.

Now in my early seventies, if I were asked which moment was most significant in my life, my answer would be the day I met my son. Unbeknownst to me at the time, this day turned me into a survivor. Suddenly, protecting him, allowing him to thrive, meant watching out for myself and making decisions that would propel us forward.

Becoming a parent helped me see why people risk their lives and put their pride aside. When you become a parent, you are not only your own child's guardian but also a stakeholder in the generation to come. When I see refugees coming into the airport circled by their children, when I see them going to work at five in the morning and returning after dark, and when I see them folding laundry for a living when they used to perform cardiac surgery, I know we are all custodians of the precious little lives we have made a promise to ourselves to steward.

Certainly not all refugees escape persecution and come to the United States for the same reasons. Some refugees don't even have children, so the reasons they cite in answer to why they came here are different from mine.

All I can say is the single most important moment in my life occurred the day I became a mother. I believe motherhood is the most powerful confluence of compassion, vision, strength, vulnerability, and single-mindedness that, when summoned, will win out against ideology, outlast war, and ensure one generation's ability to set another one up on its legs.

I believe in the power of motherhood and its ability to withstand crushing pressure, painful onslaughts, and desperate circumstances from one end of the world to another. I believe this because I have seen African, Asian, and Cuban mothers kiss their babies' faces the same way I kissed mine.

Like them, I saved my son, and then I taught him how to survive. From me he learned life humbles us when we least expect it. From me he learned that one's pain can be channeled into good. Yes, history will likely forget us, but we still count.

I believe my work helped save me. I help those longing to be seen, to be heard, and in so doing I find my own voice. My work gives me the chance to shove my face up into that of Misery's, rattle my finger, and say, "Okay, you won. You changed my course, but I will create the path from here. I will direct the sails of this ship."

I believe embedded inside every refugee is the story of how ordinary people become extraordinary. The story of how, in a moment's time, one lights a fire within oneself and says "*No.*" The story, most especially, of how we sneak up on Misery, tap him on the shoulder, and with a twinkle in our eye let out a big belly laugh. How, against his shocked face, we plant our heel, spin around, and walk away as champions.

978-0-595-43908-9
0-595-43908-X

Printed in the United States
94332LV00003B/424-462/A